Twilight Mystery

Emma Raven

Twilight Mystery

Typeset by Roberta L. Melzl
Editor: Bobbie Chase
Printed in Germany, 2008

ISBN: 1-933343-76-1

Stabenfeldt, Inc.
457 North Main Street
Danbury, CT 06811
www.pony4kids.com

Available exclusively through PONY Book Club.

Chapter 1

The trailer sped on, taking us down the last stretch of highway. I looked at the white lane lines rushing past and felt a drowsiness creeping up on me from the droning sound of the engine. Through sleepy eyes, I looked around at the others.

Ryan was in front of me in the front passenger seat, asleep with his head angled gently against the headrest. A lock of his black hair teased over the top. Ryan's dad, Mr. Vazquez, drove on beside him, like a machine. He was used to taking the horses on long journeys, but this must sure take some beating on him. I glanced down at my watch. It was four o'clock. We'd been driving for five hours and it was our second day of traveling.

According to Mr. Vazquez's minute-perfect schedule, we would arrive at 6:30. I gazed at the back of Ryan's brown neck. He was gorgeous: tall but not too skinny, olive skinned with nice cheekbones and great eyebrows. Part of me wished that I could just stay half-asleep, staring at Ryan and feeling the excitement and nerves beginning to bubble up inside me – because we were on the trip of a lifetime – to a movie set!

The horses were quiet in the trailer behind us. I thought of Luce, my black beauty, standing there with the others, with his beautiful knowing eyes and coat like satin. Was he wondering whether this journey was ever going to end? It would be the farthest he had ever been from home. We'd been taking turns checking, feeding and watering them. If that wasn't enough, we could watch them on closed-captioned TV! The transporter was really huge and the best you could buy. It even had air conditioning for the horses. They were all very happy the last time I'd been back to check.

I turned to my friend Rachel, beside me in the back passenger seat, and she was ready with a smiling face. She'd probably been laughing at me staring at her brother!

"Can't be far now," she said, "another two hours maybe?"

I grinned at her and nodded as Ryan opened his eyes and took in a deep breath.

"How far, Dad?" he asked.

✻   ✻   ✻   ✻

Five months ago…

Ryan and I had just turned Luce and Red out into the field when Mr. Vazquez called us in from the back door of the house.

"Come to the living room."

I turned around from our usual end-of-the-day position, resting my arms on the top bar of the gate, as Rachel and Liv, her blonde, petite best friend, emerged from the tack room.

We all reluctantly responded to Mr. Vazquez's summons.

"Come on!" he called impatiently, making several large sweeping movements with his arm to gather us through the door. I thought I saw the smallest hint of a smile cross his serious features. Ryan must have seen it too because we looked at each other and frowned, then grinned before sprinting to the back door of the long house.

Liv and Rachel piled in behind us and we all sat properly on the massive sofas in the living room, like we were in class waiting for an announcement.

Mr. Vazquez was over at his desk with his back to us. The surface was covered in papers, his printer busily churning out more sheets. He turned around to face us.

"A summer job has finally been confirmed," he said. "I'll be away for ten days and I'll be taking all of them with me." He gestured out of the big window to the horses in the field.

"All"? – did he really mean Luce too? Luce had never been taken on location. My mind started spinning.

"I don't know much about the movie, but the production company is big. I've worked with the Assistant Director before, but on smaller projects." Mr. Vazquez shrugged and half smirked. "This is really good for us." It was the closest he was ever going to get to looking really pleased.

"But I will need some help with this one."

I looked across the cozy, warm room to Ryan and his sister Rachel as their father turned to them.

"You two will be riding, as doubles."

I grinned excitedly at them. They were so lucky. Stunt riding. Ryan and Rachel were already pretty experienced. I could only dream of waving goodbye to the house and the woods to join them on a trip to make a movie. I'd have

7

done anything to go with them and just hang out – make coffee all day – anything, just to be there.

"For this one we need extra help."

I felt my heart skip a beat and held my breath.

"So we need you, Liv. And Salma…"

'Sorry.' That's what I'm going to hear next, 'Sorry, maybe next time.'

"You must go and ask your parents if you can come too."

I gasped and felt my mouth break into the biggest smile, first at Mr. Vazquez, who nodded to me and then across at Ryan – and Rachel. She let out a spontaneous shriek and was clapping her hands.

"Oh, this is just… this is… Dad! This is so cool!"

Ryan was nodding. His eyes caught mine for a second. I was pretty sure he was pleased. Even Liv, Ryan's ex-girlfriend who I didn't always get along with, patted me on the knee.

"When do we go?" she asked Mr. Vazquez. "I want to write it on my calendar."

"I'm going to count down the days!" Rachel cried and threw herself back into the sofa. Her immaculate brown ponytail whipped across her beautiful face.

"It looks like we will leave here at the end of June when school finishes."

I watched Rachel do the calculations. "Four months!!" she cried. "That's forever!"

"Bet it goes fast, though," Liv said, her wide, light blue eyes sparkling with excitement.

"No, it'll drag," Rachel insisted. "I can't believe Salma's coming too, though. Wow!"

"I can't believe it either," I murmured.

"It'd be funny if your parents won't let you go," Ryan

said dryly. Rachel slapped her brother playfully on the arm. "No it wouldn't."

Ryan rolled his eyes. "Joke!"

Mr. Vazquez clapped his hands together. "Now I need to look at all this paperwork in peace," he said. "Go and enjoy a little bit of sun. We haven't seen it for so long."

We didn't need to be told again, and made our way back out into the yard. Our horses were playing an energetic game in the field. I wished we could run up to them and tell them what we'd just heard, and for them to react as excitedly as we had.

Across from the stables, nestling at the far end of the field under the trees was my house where I lived with my mom and dad – and Tony, who worked in my parents' business. He was my friend now, and he was also Rachel's boyfriend. It was a shame we'd be leaving him behind.

I reached the gate and resumed my lazy slouch across the top bar, and Ryan was suddenly next to me again. Perfectly, Luce, my wonderful black stallion, together with Ryan's young chestnut stallion Red, cantered across the field. The two stopped right in front of us, and then both stood stock-still, like statues, and stared at us.

Ryan and I laughed.

"They've been practicing," I said.

Ryan grinned "And we'll be practicing a whole lot more once Dad tells us what we've got to do."

I nodded. I felt a swell of pride and love come over me as I looked at Luce and wondered what was in store for us. I couldn't imagine life without him. He eyed me and snorted, staring down to the side – a little affectation he had. I wished I could tell him the news about the summer trip. I had been working on a few tricks with him, and my horse gymnastics were really coming along. I wondered if there would be any stunts for any of us to do this time.

"What was the movie? I can't remember anything your Dad said now!" I laughed.

Ryan shrugged. "Don't know. But if we can get the working title and the director's name I can find out. Dad's not very good at getting that kind of info. He's just about the horses and what we have to do."

"Let's have a look later," I said excitedly as Luce stamped the hard, frosted ground, demanding our attention once again. I gazed at his solid frame and gleaming coat.

Then, in an instant, the two horses were galloping away dramatically. I giggled and looked across at my house, surrounded by the woods. I would be going back for supper in a minute and I'd ask them and they would say yes and then all I'd have to do would be to count the days and, of course, spend as much time with Ryan as possible – and Luce and Red – with a bit of school in between. The countdown had begun!

❊　❊　❊　❊

"Two hours and we should arrive," Mr. Vazquez replied from the driver's seat as the sun shone strongly through the windows of the cab. "The last hour there will be no towns, absolutely nothing."

Ryan turned around in his seat to face us. "You know it's in the middle of nowhere, don't you?"

The name of the place really gave it away. Lindenberg Castle. It didn't sound like it was next to a shopping mall.

It had to be remote, and secretly I hoped it was. Ryan and I had found an old grainy picture postcard of it on the Internet – it was a massive place – a huge square with a courtyard in the middle and turrets and coned roofs. It looked like something from a movie.

"The nearest town with any hotel is well over an hour away." Ryan went on.

"Lucky we're staying at the castle then," I told him.

"We won't stop in the town." Mr. Vazquez announced. "So, anything you don't have, Rachel – nail polish, eye shadow and whatever else you paint on yourselves, you'll have to make do!" He actually laughed to himself – a deep, "heh, heh."

"Thanks *Dad,* but we checked our makeup bags about fifty times before we left," Rachel said sarcastically.

"And if we've forgotten anything we'll just steal it from the makeup trailer," Liv added. Both girls laughed.

Ryan and his father glanced at each other and Ryan shook his head. "You're pathetic," he said, turning to look at the two girls.

"You know that Jake Sands isn't starring in the film, right?" I could tell by Ryan's tone that he knew that they didn't know. I didn't either. I had been looking forward to checking the star out myself.

Liv and Rachel gasped theatrically, and Liv brought her hand up to her mouth.

"You lie!" she said, pointing at Ryan as if she were in a courtroom drama.

Ryan faced the front again and stared at the road ahead.

"What are you talking about, Ry?" Rachel asked. Liv poked his shoulder from the seat behind. Ryan turned back irritably to face them and I leaned forward to hear what he was about to say, glad I had a less excitable character than Liv and Rachel. It would be hard to be as hysterical as they were.

"Jake Sands injured his foot a month ago and they've been waiting to see if he would recover in time. But… they've had someone else lined up for months. Sands can't do the movie now for sure," Ryan told us – and then once again turned back to face the front, almost sending the two girls diving through the narrow gap between the seats after him.

"Ry, this is not funny," Rachel shrieked.

Ryan shrugged. "Am I laughing?" he asked. He was enjoying winding us up.

"Oh please, Ry. Tell us what you know. You obviously know something, don't you?" Liv wailed.

"You could too if you learned how to search for stuff on the Internet and find interesting websites," he said, "like I did last week."

The girls groaned.

"Just tell us!" Rachel screamed.

I saw Mr. Vazquez's shoulders flinch.

"Tell them now," he said to Ryan.

Ryan didn't need another invitation.

He turned back around to the three of us. Even I felt like slapping him if he didn't spill the beans right away!

"Let's put it this way," he said. "I think you will be *very* pleased to find out who has replaced Jake Sands," he said. "The word 'idiot' springs to mind."

We all gasped now. He had to mean Benicio – Benicio Pinto, who had worked with us at the stables the summer before for a couple of days shooting the end of a movie, who Liv had had a bit of a thing with, who was only 19, and who was a spoiled fool, who made us all hate him. He was a very good-looking spoiled fool, though!

Ryan turned to face the front.

"Oh… my!" Rachel said, trying to keep her voice down. She looked from me to Liv. Liv's mouth was hanging open. Then I realized mine was too. I never thought I would see Benicio Pinto again. He was last year's big Hollywood thing – and would be a big star for a while to come if he didn't make too many bad movies.

"He's already there." Ryan told us.

Liv started to whisper to her best friend. Leaving them to it, I looked out of my window and thought about the other five passengers behind us – my two favorites Luce and Red, as well as our twin bays Chokky and Velvet – and finally, the leader of our pack, Toby – a huge, gentle, gray.

It was the longest time Luce had traveled anywhere in a trailer. The others were much more used to it. They all had plenty of space though, and with Mr. Vazquez's network of friends all over the place, last night we had enjoyed a stay at a wonderful riding center.

I had led Luce down the ramp the night before, into the fresh air and he let out a triumphant announcement of his arrival. We all got to work getting the horses' food and water. There was a lovely early evening warmth after another hot day as we turned them all out into their own huge field. Ryan and I watched as Luce and Red took off to the far corner.

"He's traveling wonderfully," Ryan said.

"This time tomorrow we'll be there," I said wistfully. "Eighty bedrooms… a swimming pool, state of the art stable complex, a gym… And this is someone's house?!"

Ryan nodded. "The owner is a bit eccentric to say the least," he said. "Or crazy, whichever. He's definitely incredibly rich though. He has a son our age who's bound to be a complete weirdo if he grows up in a place like that…"

As we sped along the final stretch of the highway I started wondering for the first time what it was really going to be like working on a movie set. Unfortunately there weren't any difficult stunts to perform, although sometimes things changed at the last minute. It would just be riding, and a few shots of people talking while mounting up.

Luce and Red would be fine taking part in a racing gallop with all the other horses in the main scene. Still, I got a pang of nervousness for them – and myself, and all of us, and then the magical rush of anticipation again… and then I must have fallen asleep because the next time I looked out of the window the trailer was bumping through some enormous stone gateposts and into a magnificent tree lined drive. We had arrived!

Chapter Two

"Oh wow! This is something else," Liv said. She wasn't wrong. We were all just staring out the window in amazement.

The linden trees lining the driveway soon became a dense wood of mature trees, with pretty silver birches filling the gaps between them. I already loved it, feeling instantly at home because my own house lay nestled below tall trees. Up ahead I could see a gap and we emerged at the edge of a beautiful lake, its water like greenish-blue glass, stretching off into the distance.

"Where's the castle?" Rachel asked as we continued along the gravel road and over a ridge. Then, suddenly the castle was there in front of us. A real castle. The three of us girls leaned forward to stare out of the front window of the trailer, like we were on a school bus. I realized I had my hand clamped on Mr. Vazquez's shoulder and released my grip.

"Thank you, Salma," he said.

Ryan whistled through his teeth.

"It looks twice as big as it did on that postcard," he said.

The road was leading us down one side of the huge building. At the four corners of the castle were wonderful round turrets with conical roofs in gray slate, and iron spires pointing up from their tops. I remembered these well from the postcard. The long sides of the castle were peppered with jutting round windows and half turrets, some of which carried on up and through to the next floor, and sometimes through to the big sloping roof to make little cones. It was the most intricate building I had ever seen – and the most breathtaking. The walls were covered in a very sharp-looking light gray masonry and there was a very polished, new look to the whole thing.

As we drew closer I noticed a patio running along the facing side I'd been studying. Lawns sloped down and away from it. The patio had sets of chairs and tables, with red umbrellas at their centers. People were sitting at them. In fact, it was packed with groups of people. I craned around to have a look at the faces as we passed by. Then a wave of nerves overtook me.

The trailer rolled along down the side to the front entrance. The large white doors in the long wall were opened inwards, giving everything a friendly feel. Then we passed an archway and I got a glimpse of the inner courtyard. I peered in at the ivy-covered walls as we passed, nearly banging heads with Rachel as she did the same and we giggled.

Ahead, the gravel drive finally came to an end at another archway leading through to the stables. The trailer slotted easily through the archway into an immaculate and spacious yard. As the engine cut out there was a moment of stunned silence among us all. Just for a few seconds nobody moved and nobody spoke.

In that moment I felt something a little strange. For a split second, I thought that we should all stay in the trailer. We were safe in here. I didn't want to think that, but I did. I shook my head, like I was trying to shake the thought away. But then the strange feeling took on a bit more shape and something clicked in my head. We were being watched.

I grabbed my backpack and stared up at the towering castle wall as I leapt down from the cab. A movement instantly caught my eye. A figure – a woman in a white apron, looking down from a window high up on the roof. I raised my hand to shield my eyes from the strong sunlight, but she was gone.

Luce nearly knocked me over as I led him down the ramp, coming gently at first then skidding down and arriving in the yard with a real flourish. I saw Mr. Vazquez raise an eyebrow out of the corner of my vision and I led Luce across the flagstones toward one of the beautifully prepared stalls. I breathed in the freshly laid straw bedding, a wonderful scent, and tied the lead rope to the brand new looking ring next to the stable door. Luce shuffled to the side as I stood back, tugging on the rope slightly. He was eyeing me and I went to him and stood so his head hung over my shoulder. I spoke to him softly as his warm breath rhythmically hit my cheek. "New place, boy, for me too. And we're going to be fine, aren't we? " Luce snorted a response and stamped once as Ryan came up with his feed.

"Is he okay?"

I nodded and smiled. "Think so. It's all so, well, new. How are the others?"

"Fine," Ryan told me. "I've checked the field out.

Secure and huge, like everything else here. There's a running stream with a gravel bed. Just perfect. We'll settle them in down there to stretch their legs and then they'll come in tonight." He nodded to the far corner of the yard where there was a gap. A trail led toward the field Ryan had just told me about. Luce was going to be in the end stable, next to the opening. Red would be in the stable beside him and then Chokky, Velvet and finally Toby. All in the same row. The yard was a traditional square of stalls with the high castle wall making up one of the four sides.

Luce dug into his feed energetically as we busied ourselves and took orders from Mr. Vazquez for unloading equipment from the trailer to put it into the beautiful tack room, which had an adjoining office.

I heard the sound of hooves on the trail and looked across at Rachel, who made a face and shrugged. A magnificent Appaloosa arrived in the yard with its middle-aged male rider, who halted over by the tack room, swung himself out of the saddle and greeted Mr. Vazquez enthusiastically. Our horses and the newcomer acknowledged each other with a chorus of whinnies. Mr. Vazquez beckoned us over.

"This is Hans. He'll be helping us for the week."

The man smiled broadly at us all with crinkly eyes. He looked like one of those incredibly nice people, with a ready smile on his slightly craggy weathered face.

"I'll be showing you to your rooms when you're ready," he said excitedly. "I bet you're dying to get a look inside the castle!"

"You bet!" Rachel said, for all of us.

We all smiled at each other.

"There's a welcoming party on the patio," Hans told us. "And there's food too," he added.

I looked at the others standing around in the circle. Everyone seemed slightly nervous, but we couldn't hide in the stables any longer. It was time to meet everyone else.

"If you need anything, I'm your man," said Hans. He looked like someone who wasn't used to seeing many people. I guessed he was more excited than we were by all the arrivals.

"Is that your horse?" Liv asked.

Hans shook his head. "Domino is Alex's – the Count's son. He's been busy today welcoming people with his father."

He must be the "weirdo" Ryan had mentioned. I bet I could spot him a mile off.

"He's about your age, so it will be nice for him to have some other young people around. Anyway," Hans clapped his hands together and rocked back and forth on his feet, "you finish up here and make sure you're happy with everything. Then I'll show you to your rooms."

We lingered, watching the horses exploring their field as the light faded. Luce and Red seemed eager to make friends with Domino. Then we brought them in for their first night. The stables appeared to be ours. Apart from Hans, no one else had wandered through. We had our own space and were about to leave it and meet at least a hundred movie people – scary! I turned away from Luce and the other horses and we headed back into the yard.

Hans was waiting, smiling. We followed him toward a door in the castle wall.

There was a spotless hallway on the other side with a polished flagstone floor and some red carpeted stairs

20

leading upwards. Hans led the way up the stairs. There was a lovely old building smell. We emerged on a spacious landing overlooking the courtyard. If we'd been on our own we would have been talking, chatting away and pointing things out enthusiastically, like the coat of armor that stood between two windows.

We followed Hans up another flight of stairs that led directly off the landing, up to another identical area.

"This is the easiest way for you to come in and out from the stables." Hans told us.

"You'll probably get lost a few times, but don't worry because everybody who comes here does. You'll eventually find your way!" he laughed. Liv let out a polite laugh in response to his attempt at humor, which sounded silly, and Rachel and I giggled at her for a couple of seconds before Ryan nudged me to stop.

Hans led us up more red stairs and then another narrower flight. There were rows of doors leading off the passage to the right and the courtyard now seemed very far below us.

"Señor," Hans addressed Mr. Vazquez. "You can look down at the stables from your room here." He opened the door and gestured for Mr. Vazquez to enter. The room was vast. If a guest room up at the top of the house was this big, how palatial could the family rooms possibly be on the floors below?

"You four," he turned to smile at us, "follow me."

I knew what we were all thinking. Mr. Vazquez's room wasn't going to be right next to ours. I felt Rachel nudge me rather hard with a sharp elbow and I did the same back to her as we moved on along the passage and around the

21

corner of the castle. Another steep flight of red carpeted stairs later, and we followed Hans through to a landing.

"Bathroom." Hans pointed to the room nearest the window.

"You can choose which bedrooms you want." Liv wasted no time and rushed to the doorway closest to her.

"This one's mine," she cried from inside. "It's fantastic! I saw it first."

Hans grinned at the three of us who were left standing politely in front of him.

"Meet me in half an hour by the suit of armor, then. Hope you like your rooms," he looked at his watch. "It's probably not the right time for ghosts yet." He smiled as we all stared at him rather nervously, turned and left.

Rachel waited a couple of seconds before jumping up and down and clapping her hands together. "He's just joking," she said dismissively. "This. Is. Crazy!!!" she cried as she spun on her heel and dove for the door nearest to her. "I'll take this one." She put her head around the door. "No I won't because it's the bathroom." I burst out laughing and headed for the door next to the room Liv had claimed.

"May I suggest we all calm down," Ryan said. I turned and rolled my eyes at him. "Yes, Dad!" I replied.

My room was lovely with a bed, a half-wardrobe and a bedside table. Another door revealed an *en-suite* shower room. I heard Liv wailing out on the landing and ignored it until she came flying into my room, took one look at the door that went through to the shower, wailed again and left.

"I've got the smallest room! Anyone want to swap?" she yelled out.

Ryan called the flattest of "No's," which made me giggle. I shut the door and set about getting the shower running.

Twenty five minutes later I was happy that the black mascara had worked its magic and regarded myself in the mirror. I'd washed my hair and it was nearly dry already. It looked nice, golden and shiny – for once. In case you're wondering, my hair is shoulder length and wavy and my eyes are dark brown. I don't usually wear makeup. I look best without it, really. Rachel and Liv, on the other hand, are obsessed with makeup and hair. Rachel's eyebrows look like she's just had them done in a salon and she always wears makeup – not much though because she's beautiful. Liv wears tons of makeup on special occasions. I wondered how much she would be pasting on for the evening ahead.

I knocked on Ryan's door and he yelled "come in." The room was the same as mine but Ryan had kept it a lot tidier in the short time he'd made himself at home there.

"Have you got a shower room too?" I asked conspiratorially.

Ryan was checking himself in the mirror, something I'd never seen him do before.

He tried to hide a grin and nodded. I took advantage of the fact that he couldn't see me looking at him and gazed at his profile for a moment – the good line of his nose and the way his hair curled around his ear. He was drop-dead handsome, and he may not have been my boyfriend, but I would have been devastated if anyone else claimed him.

Suddenly, I wondered how many good looking girls there would be downstairs who, unless there was something wrong with them, would go for Ryan. I tried to put the thought out of my mind and decided, then and there, as I stared at him for a second longer, that whatever happened, I would be cool about it and hopefully there would be some nice boys down there for me too!

23

Ryan turned around to look at me. I saw his eyes widen for a moment as he looked at my face and then down at my tiered skirt.

"You're wearing a skirt, Salma. Are you all right?" I nodded and laughed.

"You look nice," he added. Rachel and Liv burst in as I felt my face deciding whether it should go red or not. Saved, we all headed out of our little apartment, down the steep stairs and around the corner of the castle. It was easy to find our way back to the first landing, where the suit of armor stood proudly and Mr. Vazquez was waiting in front of one of the courtyard windows.

Hans emerged smiling from the large door at the other end of the landing.

"Ah!" he said "Been waiting for me long?" We shook our heads as he approached.

"Everything okay with the rooms?"

"Great!" Rachel told him.

"Could not be better," Mr. Vazquez added.

Hans smiled his crinkly-eyed smile. "Wonderful. Wonderful!" Now it's my pleasure to take you down to the main hall where the Count and his wife are waiting."

We followed him back through the door. Beyond it were more red-carpeted passageways with rooms off them, and eventually we emerged at another grand landing. There were suites of furniture set out in the large space, which extended to another corner of the castle – like a huge hotel lobby. From here, we could see out onto the lawns that we'd passed on our way in. A wide staircase took us down to the hallway. The biggest chandelier I'd ever seen in my life hung as the centerpiece, and through an archway lay a grand hall of the sort I'd only ever seen in historical movies. It was packed with people.

Rachel put on a slightly nervous face as we headed toward the hall. Hans took us to the large table where drinks were laid out in rows.

"Soft drinks for you youngsters there," Hans said, smiling. "The Count is eager to meet you, Señor," he said to Mr. Vazquez.

All the tall French doors out onto the patio were open and we headed out through the nearest one, happy to be away from the noise of all the people talking in the room. The first person I laid eyes on as we stepped outside onto the patio was Benicio Pinto. He was sitting at one of the tables with four other men wearing bomber jackets and sunglasses. He turned as the five of us emerged and to my surprise he smiled and raised a hand. Liv and Rachel were smiling back and were trying to whisper at each other at the same time. We moved toward him, as I felt my heart beginning to hammer in my chest. Mr. Vazquez led the way. As we passed the table, two of Benicio's bodyguards stood and adopted a night-club doorman stance. Mr. Vazquez was oblivious to this and walked straight past them. We followed, ignoring Benicio and his cronies.

Finally finding some space we formed a circle. Mr. Vazquez stared out across the lawns.

"You stay away from that idiot," he said calmly. "He showed last year when he came to film that he is one of the worst people."

We couldn't argue with that. Benicio had been a complete nightmare the summer before. He was such a disappointment, after the excitement of knowing that he was coming. Then there had been the flirty thing with Liv – I didn't really know what had happened. I decided that I wasn't going to have anything to do with Benicio. It was a shame, though. Even where we were standing, his aura felt like royalty. He was looking very good, too. His hair was short and deliberately messy and his tanned skin looked perfect. The four bodyguards sitting there watching him were a truly sad sight, but it had been the same when he'd come to film the scenes with us. We weren't going to give him the satisfaction of trying to get close to him.

Then I saw Ryan smile and head into the hall. The man who gave Ryan a warm hug looked about thirty and was very good looking.

"Oh, it's Steven!" Rachel cried, giving a cute little wave. The man was already coming over to us. He had an assured look that I feared everyone in the packed room had, with the exception of myself. Steven kissed Rachel on both cheeks.

"Hello beautiful," he said. "Good to see you again."

His hair was a bit messy, but probably intentionally so, and his teeth were perfect, a dazzling white. He shook hands with Mr. Vazquez.

"And you, sir," he said politely. Everyone talked to Mr. Vazquez like that, showing tremendous respect.

"We're glad to be working with you," Mr. Vazquez replied.

Rachel put an arm around my shoulder.

"This is Salma," she said, "and this is Liv."

I smiled, trying to rid my expression of the shyness I was sure it betrayed.

"Hello."

Liv was straight in there.

26

"Hi, I've heard all about you," she bubbled, "Aren't you the Assistant Director?"

Steven's smile became even wider.

"Sure am."

We all looked at each other for a moment, nodding and smiling.

"Quite a location we have here, don't you think?"

"It's fabulous," Rachel agreed.

I felt myself zoning out of the polite chat. It was difficult to hear everyone properly anyway. As the chatter in the room became louder, everyone raised their voice even more. Steven was talking again, semi-shouting now. Mr. Vazquez was nodding.

Then, the pinging sound of someone tapping a wine glass reached our ears and a hush began to fall over the room. The faces slowly turned around to the top of the room, opposite the grand archway where we had entered. There, standing on a raised platform, was a strange looking middle-aged man. I'd tried to imagine the Count and hadn't gotten very far, but this had to be him. He was wearing a gray three-piece suit, was slightly overweight and sported an old-fashioned combed-over hairstyle like a character out of an old film. His hair was jet black and his features were large. His two front teeth seemed to protrude slightly. He was one homely man.

Rachel nudged my elbow in the usual way and I fought the urge to let out a little giggle. It was time to act more mature. Our group moved to the side of the room and a little forward, finding some space almost in front of the raised platform that you could imagine a string quartet playing on.

"I have no wish to keep you all from enjoying my hospitality," the Count began in a commanding voice.

As he spoke, a petite and beautiful lady stepped up beside him, her blonde hair wavy like Marilyn Monroe had worn hers – and then a teenager around our age. He had to be the son and he wasn't what I expected.

"I wish to welcome you all here to Lindenberg Castle and hope that your stay will be one to remember. As you can see, our refurbishment is complete, and if there is anything we can do to make you more comfortable, please don't hesitate to bring it to our attention."

Count Silverberg was like an eccentric headmaster. I listened and suddenly got the feeling someone was looking at me. My eyes flicked to the side.

"My wife and my son Alex are so proud to see this day come…"

Alex! Well, he certainly didn't look like the weirdo Ryan had predicted. Short, sandy hair – a beautiful chiseled face which his features softened. He clearly took after his mother. His eyes were light blue or green, but I couldn't look for long because they were staring into mine. I caught a hint of a smile in the moment he held my gaze. I turned around to check if Rachel was behind me. It had to be her he was looking at. It was usually that way. There was no one behind me. Just the wall. I looked back at Alex. He really was looking at me. Then his gaze turned to his father.

"Thank you for coming, and we look forward to meeting you all over the coming week."

The Count beamed at his audience. Speech over, there were murmured thank you's as the three of them stepped down from the platform and were lost in the throng. The room was suddenly noisy again as everyone picked up their conversations.

I turned back to our group and felt a jolt at the sight of a sleek, flame-haired girl hugging Ryan. She leaned back out of the hug but kept her arms clasped around his waist. Ryan was grinning at her, whoever she was. She seemed to be thrilled to see him.

"Look at you – as gorgeous as ever! I hoped it might be you guys as soon as I saw the script." I glanced at Liv. She was watching, like me. Ryan slipped his arm around her shoulder and turned around to the group.

"Guys, this is Sandy," he said.

Sandy showed us her great set of teeth.

"Which one's your girlfriend?" she asked, laughing for no reason. "None, I hope!" she shrieked.

Ryan shook his head. "I was waiting to see you again, of course."

I felt a bolt of something strong shoot through me. I don't think it was jealousy. He wasn't my boyfriend, so how could I be! I'd never seen Ryan act all cheesy before and I wasn't used to it. I felt nervous and all wrong, standing there clutching my glass. I'd finished the cranberry juice ages ago. I watched Ryan and Sandy clutching each other and smiling widely. Who on earth was Sandy anyway? It was all so fake.

Mr. Vazquez had drifted across the room with Steven – and Liv and Rachel were deep in conversation. I leaned in to Rachel.

"Back in a sec," I said into her ear. I was ready with a smile when she looked at me. She nodded and I turned and headed for the nearest French doors. I knew that Ryan hadn't even noticed me leaving.

29

I stood for a few seconds out on the patio in the dark. Everyone seemed to feel that the place to be was inside. I don't ever cry but I thought about it right then and took a deep breath before heading along the patio – wishing I hadn't when I noticed Benicio and his crew still out there around the last table. I looked down until I passed by his chair and smiled.

"Nice to see you again, Salma," he said in a half-American, half-Italian accent. I nearly tripped over thin air! I doubted he'd even remember me, let alone remember my name!

"And you," was my over-polite star-struck reply. There was no way I was stopping at the table to make a fool of myself so I walked on quickly to the corner of the castle, rounding one of the huge turret bases. I turned left down the long side where the main entrance was and on toward the stables. I walked the fifty yards down the driveway purposefully as the gravel crunched under my shoes.

My way was lit by little pools of yellow light from the porch lamps and the cozily lit rooms within. Outside though, the darkness from the surrounding forest felt close, and it was quiet and eerie. My mind wandered back to what Hans has said about the ghosts.

As I neared the archway, the Count's words echoed in my mind.

"Your stay will be one to remember."

I knew it would be, somehow.

Passing under the arch a sound made me stop in my tracks: the snapping of a bolt of a door being rammed open split the night air and I ran into the yard, as Luce's piercing whinny rang out into the night.

The yard was deserted so I slowed and scanned the

stalls. Luce stood with his head hanging over the door. He whinnied a greeting to me as I approached but it sounded wrong. His eyes were all over the place and his ears flicked backwards. When I was a few yards away from him, his half door began to yawn outwards. I rushed forward and caught it when it was about a foot open. Luce was just about to push it wide open after the initial gentle pressure he'd used to get the door moving. I pushed it back and fumbled for the bolt, leaning my whole weight against the door. The bolt was already completely across, which must have been the sound I had heard. I pulled it back, slammed the half door with all my might and smashed the bolt back again into its latch. Red kicked his half-door – agitated by the sudden flurry of activity.

I couldn't believe what had just happened and how I'd sprung into action in that split second. My heart pounded in my chest. Luce was now skittering around in his stall. He whinnied again and came forward. His features were on full alert and his usual slightly naughty demeanor gone. He was trying to fight it, but he was frightened. Struggling to take everything in, I grasped his nose and muzzle and rested my head against his silky cheek. I whispered soothingly into his ear. Luce breathed heavily and I felt him start to relax. He was intelligent enough to know that the danger was over. I didn't want to think about what would have happened if I hadn't come to see him. Who on earth had messed around with the bolt? Red seemed calm now too. I closed my eyes and looked back at Luce. And then I felt a hand on my shoulder.

31

Chapter Three

I spun around and stifled a scream as I found Benicio staring at me.

It took a second to catch my breath and I prayed I wouldn't have a heart attack.

"Sorry! Sorry, Salma! I just wanted to check that you were all right."

I looked up at his face and just stared at him. Was he really there? Surely not. One of the biggest acting stars in the world with me in the dark courtyard and apparently checking if I was okay?!

It was like I'd gotten out of my seat in the movie theater and walked up to the screen. I'd seen him in the flesh the summer before and he was in great shape then. He looked even better now. There was a big difference though, as if the arrogant expression that had dominated his features then seemed to have been replaced by something else – something nicer.

"You looked kind of upset."

Benicio still had his hand on my shoulder, his arm

crossing the space between us. His eyes, wonderful and twinkling in the near dark, stared into mine.

I jumped as Luce kicked his door and snorted.

"Someone was here. I heard him messing around with the bolt on Luce's door." I gestured behind me.

Benicio looked over his shoulder and walked up to Luce's half door.

"Hey," he said slowly. "How could I forget you." I felt a massive swell of pride as Luce shook his head restlessly but then settled and allowed Benicio to stroke his nose.

"You sure?" he said, turning back to me. "Any idea where they went?"

I decided it was time to come out of my Hollywood-induced trance.

"Maybe around the corner." I offered. "It's the only way out, besides the archway."

Benicio had his head resting against Luce's neck.

My horse playfully nuzzled into Benicio's shoulder and then pushed him gently.

Benicio broke away and looked around the corner toward the paddock and the woods beyond.

"Shall we go and check?" he whispered. "Come on."

He took my hand and we half ran out of the courtyard, passing the trailer over on the right of the gap. Hugging the wall, we crept around the back of the stable block. I followed Benicio's lead and thought about his hand holding mine. The excitement of it was almost too much to bear on top of everything else. We stopped and stood there in the dark.

We could see that the field was empty. The woods started at the far end and swept around on either side close

33

to the fence so that from behind the stable block, the first line of trees was only a few yards away. It was possible to see into the forest a little way, but it would be easy to run in and disappear quickly.

The forest was pitch black and scary. Benicio took the words right out of my mouth.

"I don't want to go in there."

He leaned back against the wall.

"Are you okay? You looked strange when you passed me."

I nodded. The nerve-wracking atmosphere of the reception suddenly seemed like years ago. Things had gone way past there in the unreal stakes!

"It's a bit crazy, you know." I shrugged and continued whispering. "All these people and this place. I've never been on a set before. They all seem so sure of themselves. Did you ever feel like that?" I cursed myself for babbling.

Benicio chuckled.

"When I got my first big part. I was afraid to talk to anyone," he said, "and then within about two weeks of the movie being released everyone started treating me like a god – always in my face. 'Do you want this or that?' Designers sending me clothes and begging me to wear them. It does things to you…" His face became solemn. "Then my mom got ill last year," he paused. I put my hand on his arm, wondering how we'd gotten into such a conversation. "She's okay now," he went on, "but she told me she didn't know me anymore. It was hard to take, you know, from your mother." He let out a little laugh. "Sorry, Salma. I didn't mean to put all that on you. But what I mean is… that it's strange being in a place like this. I'd do anything these days not to have four guys around me the whole time like some life support machine. My assistant can't be here this week so it's just them and I can't even talk to them. Now my agent thinks I should have a nutritionist!"

I giggled as he let out a hissing laugh.

We were silent for a moment staring into the woods.

"I want to see your horses again," Benicio said. "Whoever was here is gone, I think."

I nodded and we turned to retrace our steps along the back of the stable block.

Then the sound of wood snapping cracked out of the woods. I felt a bolt of terror in my chest as we both spun around. Someone was hiding in the trees. Benicio looked at me in alarm. We stared back at the trees for a second and then hurried back to the yard.

Luce snorted as we rounded the corner and then Benicio clutched my arm again because we weren't alone. The yard lights were on and a figure emerged from behind Luce's head. Ryan.

"Salma!" He looked from me to Benicio and then back to me, clearly surprised and wondering what on earth was going on.

As I opened my mouth, I knew it was going to come out wrong.

"Someone was in the stable yard."

I saw a switch flick in Ryan's head as he stepped forward and the lights showed his sour looking face.

"We're going for a ride with the Count's son tomorrow morning," he told me, curtly. "Make sure you're not late."

He turned and strode across the yard to the door in the castle wall.

"Great!" That was the sarcastic thought that I would fall

35

asleep thinking, too. I didn't go after Ryan and I didn't see him again afterwards.

I left Benicio and found Mr. Vazquez and told him about the incident with Luce's door. I kind of left out the part about being with Benicio. It was enough to know Mr. Vazquez believed me and would make sure the horses were safe – he'd sleep in the trailer.

Rachel grabbed me when I finally showed up in the hall again and I took my chance to have some food. I got the low-down on everyone they had spoken to in the room since I'd left. Sandy was in her first co-starring role and apparently was a complete ditz. They had worked on a small film with her before. Steven, the assistant director, was crazy about Rachel, and Liv was certain that Benicio would be an even bigger idiot than he had been the summer before and she wasn't interested in him any more.

The hall emptied slowly as it got late and we ambled back to the wonderful main staircase. I listened to the others' enthusiastic chatter and tried not to be bothered that Ryan was in a bad mood because of me.

"That Alex, the son," Liv whispered as we reached the first floor lounge area where a few guests had settled for late night conversation, "he's kind of good looking." We giggled together. I was glad to be back with them. "See you tomorrow morning," she added. I was looking forward to the ride too. Apparently, Alex would be showing us the woods and telling us about the castle. I couldn't wait! We'd be with the horses all day too.

As I lay in the wonderfully comfortable bed I realized my nervousness was gone and I couldn't wait for the morning, the film set and the whole thing to start.

Ryan was moody at breakfast in the dining room through the main hall. I tried to smile at him a couple of times but he ignored me. Rachel asked me what I thought his problem was and I just shook my head in reply.

Ryan wouldn't have told them about finding me with Benicio and I wasn't about to share this with Liv and Rachel because they would just start screaming and I could hardly believe it had happened myself.

I'd let them find out for themselves that Benicio was a surprise – that is, if last night hadn't been a strange fluke.

I'd forgotten my long-sleeved shirt and had to go back up to get it from my room. By the time I got back down, Ryan had started to saddle Luce up. It wasn't lost on me that he was implying that I was late. I took the saddle from him without a word and he went back to Red, who was ready to go, and he mounted up. It wasn't the time to talk about ghosts, but if he kept up this bad mood with me I'd definitely tell him there was one in his room.

The thought made me laugh and I was aware of Alex over on the other side of the yard with his horse, Domino, the fabulous Appaloosa stallion we'd seen the evening before. Up close, Domino looked awesome. He had an all over mottled pattern. His head and front quarters were bay with white flecks – giving way to white over the back and hips with large brown and black spots. He was very compact with a great shaped neck. I could see the power in his limbs. He was a real stunner.

I hadn't met Alex yet. He walked Domino over and started chatting to Ryan. Then he nodded to me with a smile.

Mr. Vazquez appeared and told us that we had to be in a

meeting with the director, Jonathan, at one o'clock to run through our main shot for the day after tomorrow. Ryan and Rachel were due for test makeup at four o'clock for their doubling roles. Then he casually told me that at five o'clock I had to go there too and then on to costume because I would be riding Luce as an extra. I tried to take the news calmly but a smile broke out from the corners of my mouth. I was actually going to be in the film, riding in the background in a scene where Benicio and Sandy's characters go out for a ride! The scene was to involve a short race between the two, and that was where Ryan and Rachel came in. They would double for the flat-out long shots. Mr. Vazquez would have a few days to work with Benicio and Sandy – and Velvet and Toby, their mounts for the standing and racing shots, to ensure all horses and riders were comfortable with each other.

I figured Mr. Vazquez was in for a better time with Benicio than the summer before.

I mounted up and Ryan and Red were suddenly next to us.

"Dad told me about last night." he said, with a hint of an apology.

I nodded.

"We'll have to keep our eyes open in case there's something weird going on."

"I tried to tell you…"

"I know," he cut in.

We were all ready to go. Alex joined our huddle in the middle of the yard. Liv was on Chokky and Rachel on Velvet.

"Beautiful horse you have there," he said to me, "Amazing strength in his hindquarters – and I like the look in his eye."

Luce tossed his head, like a cheeky acknowledgement of

the compliment. I could tell he was itching to leave the yard and stretch his legs as we moved off, out of the back corner of the yard through the gap at the corner. Alex and I led the way.

"I've never seen horses in such beautiful condition as yours," Alex said. "Ryan tells me your boy can be a handful at times."

"He sure can," I agreed. "He's been called headstrong and obstinate, but I'd say it's no more than a little mischief and a sense of humor."

Alex raised an eyebrow. "You're probably not wrong with that look he has. As soon as I saw him he reminded me of Domino. That look that makes you think he knows everything."

I looked at Alex in a way that said I knew exactly what he meant. He was so friendly – and confident. The way he spoke was quite formal but that didn't bother me. His face was tanned and his hair sun-kissed around his face.

"Luce is a Lusitano, isn't he? I've always been a fan of them. Intelligent, gentle and affectionate. Is that right?"

I nodded. "They're awesome. Perfect for training as stunt horses. Do you ride much here?"

We were heading along the back of the stable block where Benicio and I had been the night before. I glanced into the woods to my right. They were a welcoming sight in the light of day. Like the woods on the way in, the forest was composed of very tall trees and smaller ones that looked like ash, and then clusters of silver birches. The path ahead was about to gently veer off into the trees and away from the castle.

"When I'm here, yes. Every day. All day!" he laughed. "I'm away at school, you see. Hans rides Domino for me during school time. I was so pleased when I found out you were all coming because I would have someone to ride out with."

I'd never thought about what it would be like to have no one to ride with. I was lucky to have everyone around all the time.

"Where are you taking us today?"

"We'll do the woods. Well, that's pretty much all there is except for the lawns and the lake," he paused, "for now anyway, until my father clears a lot of it for his tennis courts or whatever he wants to do next for all the rich people who will supposedly pay a lot of money for the privilege of coming here."

There was more than a hint of disquiet in his voice.

"If you could look from the air, we're basically in the middle of the forest here. Fifty square miles of it. There are a few clearings and a lot of pathways like this, so many you could really get lost, but obviously I know them all like the back of my hand. It took me a while, though."

The path was lush and grassy – a vivid green, and as we headed into the trees the wonderful quiet of the woodland descended, interrupted by sporadic birdsong and the sound of walking hooves. Luce really was itching to go.

"Have you lived here all your life?"

Alex nodded a reply. "Do you think that's strange?"

I looked at him questioningly. It was like he was worried I might think he was odd. I remembered Ryan's "weirdo" conclusion from the journey down.

"No. It must be amazing to live here," I said enthusiastically and I meant it. "I bet there's hidden treasure and secret tunnels." It was unfortunate that I managed to sound like a seven-year-old instead of thinking of something intelligent to say, but Alex was smiling across at me.

"There's that and more," he said. I could see his pride in

his home swelling in his chest and he continued in response to my excited expression. "We've got a couple of ghosts, and somewhere in the castle is a nice little haul of precious jewels. Millions of dollars worth that someone tried to steal. Well, they *did* steal them, but they had to hide them first and they never got to come back and escape with them."

My eyes were wide with wonder at the fantastic story, and I made a mental note to ask about the ghosts too.

"Who stole them?"

"My father's younger stepbrother Philip and a maid, Sofia." Alex went on. "I know," he said, taking in my amazed expression. "It sounds like I made it up. My father realized the jewels were gone and caught my uncle in the middle of the night, the day after he'd faked a boating accident on the lake. Everyone was concentrating on trying to find a body because we thought he was dead."

Alex looked like he found the whole thing slightly funny. "Hans caught Sofia waiting with a car, oddly enough just about where we're passing now on this path. Passports, tickets and bags all ready. Uncle Philip was never going to inherit the castle so I guess it was a way out for him and his girlfriend."

"What happened to them?"

"They escaped before the police got here. Not without a fight though – with a couple of those swords you see hanging around on the walls. Hans lost an eye. They were never seen again – never caught."

I winced at the thought of the injury to poor Hans.

Alex shook his head. "Sorry. We've only just met and I'm telling you all this. It's a crazy story."

"It's great," I said. "I mean, not great, but…"

"It's nice to have people my age to talk to," Alex said

apologetically. I felt sorry for him. I guessed he had spent some long and lonely summers at the castle. His eagerness to make friends didn't make him any less appealing.

"We're glad to have the chance to come somewhere as fantastic as this and to meet you," I told him. "Let's hope we all have a fantastic time."

Alex nodded and smiled shyly.

"If I start babbling just tell me," he said.

"Who are the ghosts?"

"A maid who threw herself from the roof and broke her neck – and there's my great, great grandfather Charles too," Alex laughed.

"Are they friendly?"

"Charles is," Alex replied, "but he's only been seen five times since he died. I'm not sure about her though," he added. "People have left the castle in the middle of the night because of her." Alex made a face.

Just then Ryan came alongside. I slowed and fell in with Liv and Rachel.

"He likes you," Liv said immediately. "Doesn't he, Rach?"

Rachel nodded. "Absolutely! He was asking where you were earlier."

This news was interesting to me, but too typical of Liv and Rachel's usual "jumping to the most scandalous conclusion" style to be taken too seriously.

Rachel's sleek ponytail bobbed as she rode along on Chokky.

"Are you going to let that girl Sandy ride Velvet?" Liv asked. "I wouldn't if I were you."

Rachel and I started laughing.

"It's not like she's got much choice, is it?" I replied. Liv shrugged. "I hope Velvet shows her who's boss anyway," she said. "She already thinks she's queen of *this* set. I bet her career lasts five minutes."

I was looking forward to hearing what craziness Liv was going to come out with next, but then Rachel shouted.

"Hey!" she pointed ahead. "Look at them go!"

Alex and Ryan had taken off along the path as it opened out into a wider avenue and the three of us instantly rose into a gallop in pursuit. Luce was flying, his powerful stride instantly taking us away from the other two. We were both loving it. We came out into a huge grassy clearing, perfectly round, which we raced across and back into the woods. I could tell that the trail was roughly going around the castle, although we couldn't see the castle from where we were. We were just a bit too far away and the trees too dense. All the way around the wide grassy path other narrower paths branched off in both directions. It was like being in a gigantic maze.

Alex was smiling proudly when we joined him and Ryan at the center of a second clearing.

"We can go on up ahead," he pointed to where the path continued back into the trees on the far side.

"But the path forks after about half a mile. It's up to you which side you go. We'll all end up together again at a third clearing. Ready?"

We all answered affirmatively.

"See you in a minute, then!" Alex said cheekily, turning Domino dramatically and making for the far side of the open space. He was clearly in his element.

We all watched for a few seconds before heading off after him in a long line: Ryan first, then Liv, Rachel, and finally me. Luce was ecstatic to be pounding after his friends. This was as exciting for him as it was for me. I was totally comfortable at a full gallop after being a complete novice when we became the Vazquez's neighbors. I'd said goodbye to walking endless circles a long time ago, and boy did it feel good. My beautiful horse loved nothing better than this. As we plunged into the woods again I took in the cool sight of my friends ahead of me riding at top speed. The path curved around gently to the left, just as it had done thus far.

Ahead I could now see where it forked into two slightly narrower but still generous paths. Rachel took the one on the right and I chose the left. It had a wonderful tunnel of trees, pleasantly darker because of the canopy overhead. As it straightened out a little I saw a flash of Ryan's maroon sweatshirt a long way ahead. Two seconds later I was pulling hard on Luce's reins to draw him to a desperate halt.

Ryan was doubled over on the ground and there was no sign of Red.

We stopped dramatically just short of his stricken form.

Just then, Red came trotting back down the path from ahead and stopped alongside his master. His eyes were everywhere and his ears back.

I dismounted and rushed to Ryan's side. He was grimacing and trying to talk, but he couldn't. I put my arm around his back.

"Are you okay?"

Stupid question. I wasn't used to seeing him distressed. He was clearly winded.

"Came off…" he said, through frantic gulps for air. "Someone jumped out… deliberately… I went down like a rock… can't believe I couldn't stay on…"

He reached up to Red and began checking him over, still taking in mouthfuls of air. Red stood calmly now, as if he'd just successfully completed a stunt. That was what our horses were like – mostly – obedient and calm.

"Whoever it was… grabbed the reins and rode off on him. I saw them mount … a running mount."

"It's okay. He's back now, clever boy. He looks fine. Is he okay?" Ryan managed a nod and doubled himself over again. "Must have shaken them off, or…"

Ryan started scanning the trees on either side of the path.

"Whoever it was is still out there." Ryan mounted up with an agonizing groan of pain. "Let's get out of here."

I followed him along the trail, pleased to see that he and Red soon picked up the pace. I was relieved that Ryan was feeling okay again, but suddenly something caught my eye in the trees to my left. I pulled Luce to a halt and peered into the woods. Ryan was already out of sight ahead of me. I should have cantered on after him. But there *was* movement in the trees. A person. Two people. I peered through the broken walls of tree trunks at the moving shapes, dressed in dark colors. They weren't watching me, but were bending down and looking at something.

Then there was the sound of a quiet motor, like a moped, firing up. My first instinct was to race away. But then I had an idea. I'd seen a gap in the trees a few yards away leading to a tiny open space. And just down the trail I'd seen a large overhanging tree. I had to act quickly and line Luce up on the trail. Feeling the beginnings of a hot panic, I saw the moped beginning to move through the trees. In a moment they would be out of their hiding place – and I had better be in mine. I patted Luce's neck. He stood still waiting for the signal from me. Who said we weren't going to do any stunts on this trip!

Luce moved forward steadily as we headed for the narrow path. He knew where he was going and he would not deviate from the course I'd set him on. I felt the calm purpose in his limbs as he waited for me to do my bit. I'd practiced it for months. We crossed the path and entered the little tunnel. I rose quickly and lightly to the standing position, my arms ready to counterbalance any wobbles on the less than level saddle. I didn't need to. The branch was at chest height ahead. If I hit it too hard I'd know how Ryan had felt a few moments before. It was now or never.

I reached to hug the branch and hold on as Luce passed underneath. The hard, thick, immovable wood was a slight shock to my ribcage – but I'd made it. Another smaller branch just higher and ahead helped me scramble up. I swiveled into a crouching position on the sturdy bough and shuffled onto the trunk of the tree, feeling nicely hidden.

There wasn't time to wonder what Luce was up to. I peered back up to the trail as the sound of the moped grew. My heart thumped madly in my chest as they passed by the gap – two people together dressed in navy and black wearing helmets. I willed them not to look my way and I was in luck. All I could tell was that the one on the back of the moped had a slim figure. Not much use. One thing was for sure, though – they weren't supposed to be there.

The noise of the moped's engine trailed off slowly into the woods. I turned in the direction Luce had headed, suddenly getting a little thrill about being hidden in a tree like Robin Hood. I couldn't see him, but I knew he was there. I needed to get back to the others before they sent out a search party. I whistled – just as we had practiced back home. Luce liked doing this. He'd taken to it straight away. Immediately I heard

his hooves trotting up on the grassy floor of the path and he was there below me, in perfect position, ready for me to drop down onto his back. I hugged him and off we went.

"We'd better not tell Dad." Rachel said after we finally joined them in the third clearing and Ryan relayed what had happened.

"With this, and the thing last night, Dad will have us out of here in a flash."

We all nodded. Alex looked on gravely.

"If anything else happens though, we have to tell him," Ryan said. He'd recovered from the fall and seemed almost okay.

"Who on earth would want to knock you off your horse?" Alex said. "Everyone here is on the movie or works here."

He looked deeply puzzled. "There are guards with dogs on the perimeter as well."

"Photographers?" Rachel offered.

"Odd tactics," Ryan replied, "but you might be right."

We were all frowning, our minds awash with strange scenarios.

"They wanted Red. Whoever it was did a running mount and just took off on him."

"D'you think they're gone now?" Liv asked. She sounded scared. We all were. I couldn't believe I'd stayed to try and get a closer look at them.

"Let's get back, nice and slowly," Alex said. "We'll stay close to each other."

It was five o'clock when we all collapsed on the comfy sofas in the corner of the first floor lounge. The shock of the

48

incident on the morning ride was going away but we were all uneasy. We just couldn't figure out why anyone would feel the need to do what they had done to Ryan. What were they doing, whizzing about on a moped in the woods? And more importantly, who were they?

We'd talked though our scenes with the director. It was easy stuff and wardrobe had sorted out my very normal outfit and played with my hair. I knew I'd only be shot from a distance so it wasn't that important what I looked like. Now we were all trying to chill out.

Alex had stayed with us whenever he could. He'd been very quiet since the ride and I figured he was feeling a little responsible for what had happened to Ryan.

Rachel stood up and sighed.

"Is there a bathroom around here, Alex?"

Alex nodded. "Go through that door and then there's one, second right I think." He was pointing to the far end of the lounge, past the main staircase.

I watched Rachel walk the length of the lounge and disappear through the door. Almost as soon as she did, Mr. Vazquez appeared at the top of the stairs.

"We have to be in the hall right now," he said, in a more no-nonsense manner than usual. This was an order. He descended the stairs and we all jumped up to follow.

"What about Rach?" I said.

"I'll wait for her," Liv replied.

We entered the back of the hall. The producer – someone with an incredibly long Italian name, was speaking and everyone had gathered in front of him.

"So we will not be able to shoot any scenes in that location until we find a replacement, which should not be more than forty-eight hours, I'm hoping, at the worst. We will continue with run-throughs, and interior shots have been moved forward on the schedule. The new schedule is here." He held up a thick sheaf of papers. "It doesn't really affect most of us much. Thanks for your time, and if you have any questions ask Don." He left the platform.

"The outside caterer quit after an argument," Mr. Vazquez told us. "They need food on location because it's two miles away. We do those scenes in three days now, not the day after tomorrow. It's no matter."

I shrugged. We'd been dragged down here as if the whole project had been shelved. I scanned the faces in the room for Benicio. He wasn't there.

We slowly made our way back to the stairs and Mr. Vazquez went off with Steve.

"Where did Rachel and Liv get to?" Ryan said with a frown as we reached our sofas.

Just then Liv emerged through the door Rachel had gone through earlier. She walked quickly toward us. "Is she with you?"

"No" Ryan replied. "Did you just check the bathroom?"

Liv nodded. "She's not there."

Ryan rolled his eyes. "What next!?" he exclaimed and flopped down on the sofa.

"She was in the middle of telling me something. It's not like she would have just wandered off."

I frowned at Liv and asked, "Well, where can she be, then?"

Chapter Four

Rachel wasn't in her room, with the horses, in the hall or on the patio. We found the bathroom Alex had directed her to and she wasn't in any of the stalls. Liv even looked in the cupboards under the row of stylish glass sinks. It was a sign that we were getting a little desperate.

"Maybe she's been flushed away," Liv said, lamely attempting a joke.

We were all due at dinner so we met the others at the top of the stairs. We agreed to see if Rachel showed up at our table. If not, we'd tell Mr. Vazquez she was missing. We joined him in the long dining room off the grand hall.

"Where is Rachel?" he asked immediately.

"Just visiting Velvet and the others," Liv replied quickly, at the same time as I said, "Having a quick shower."

Liv and I looked at each other as Mr. Vazquez glared at us. He looked like he was going to say something, but instead he just glared at us both some more and shook his head. I hoped he thought that Rachel was flirting with someone in the crew and we were covering for her. The problem was that it would now be difficult to come out with the truth that she was missing in a couple of minutes, as we had agreed.

But then I turned to my right to see Rachel taking her place next to me at the table. She looked at us all and mouthed, "Tell you later," before saying, "Sorry I'm late, Dad."

I felt a big wave of relief. She looked completely fine, and as I glanced at her again I was sure she was trying to hide a grin. Alex walked through the dining room toward the hall. He noticed Rachel and kept going, smiling at me. I smiled back and looked across the table as Ryan's eyes flicked away.

We all went up to the buffet table together as was the plan, one table at a time, from the back of the room to the front. We loaded up our plates with the delicious looking food, all salads and nicely prepared cold meats, as the room began to fill up.

After the madness of the first night's reception party it seemed the crew had retreated into their little groups. I kept looking out for Benicio, but I was hardly expecting him to appear in the dining room with the rest of us. I hadn't seen Sandy again either – until the end of the meal when she draped her arms around Ryan's shoulders and stood behind him. She seemed to be suggesting riding out with us. I felt myself bristle and looked away as Rachel stood up.

"Dad, may we be excused now?"

He nodded as he took a sip of his drink, and Rachel led Liv and me through to the empty Great Hall and up the stairs, which we took two at a time.

"Our" sofas in the corner turret of the lobby were free. We made for them as the last group of stragglers from the crew pulled themselves up and headed down for dinner. Ryan hadn't followed us and I didn't care. He could stay down there for as long as he liked and be blinded by the sight of Sandy's teeth.

"Tell us before I scream," Liv whispered. "Were you with Steve?"

Rachel looked at her as if she was mental.

"Hello! I have a boyfriend, Tony. Remember him?!"

"Sorry," Liv said quietly. Usually, she would have started sulking, but her need to know what had happened to Rachel overcame her potential petulance.

"I got lost," Rachel whispered.

We leaned in toward her to listen.

"The door I thought Alex told me to go through led to a narrow corridor. I figured the bathrooms would be down at the end of it, so I kept going and opened another door at the end, but that opened out onto a weird landing. Once the door shut behind me it was pitch black. There were no windows."

"Wow!" Liv exclaimed. "So how come you didn't just come back?"

Rachel grinned.

"I could have, of course," she continued in a whisper, "but I thought I'd just take a quick look around. When I turned the lights on they lit up this maze of corridors all in really old, dark wood. Over the banister in front of me was nothing – a big drop. I walked around the one I was on and up some stairs. There was bright blue carpeting everywhere. I tell you, it's well, *weird* – like something out of a video game. I just kept on going up the stairs. I knew I should turn back but I just couldn't once I'd started. It was like no one had been in there for decades."

"So how did you get lost?" I asked her.

"I kept going 'til I got to the top. There's an immense gallery just kind of hanging in the middle and going around a room that's somewhere in the castle. It must be an immense room, though. I tried to find a door but there wasn't one, so I gave up and started to head back. I tried to go back down but it was like someone had switched it all around while I had been at the top. I tried one of the doors and there was a spiral staircase behind it. I hoped you guys would just chat away on the sofas and not realize I was taking forever."

"We might not have if we hadn't checked the bathrooms and found you weren't there. Then we started searching everywhere," I told her.

Rachel nodded. "Sorry," she said. "I decided to go down the spiral stairs. I tried a couple of doors but they were locked and I started to panic a little."

I blew out a stream of air. "So how did you get out?"

"Suddenly a door opened behind me, one I'd just tried, and this woman came through it. I nearly screamed my head off. I was like this," she gasped and put her hand over her mouth.

"The woman was *really* scary, quite old with her hair pulled back super tightly. She was dressed as a maid."

The mention of the maid sent a shiver down my back. It didn't sound as if Rachel had encountered a ghost though.

"She just said, 'Who are you?' like she owned the place, and I told her I was lost and trying to get out. She stared at me like she was trying to figure out if I was lying so I mumbled stuff about looking for the bathroom and that I was here for the film, with the horses. She gave me an even weirder look when I said that, like I'd made it up, and then she hustled me through the door into this empty room with a bed in it and no windows. Like a secret room. Then before I knew it I was shoved out onto a landing with a red carpet, and I managed to find my way back!"

Rachel looked up and stopped talking. Alex was approaching us.

"You going to tell him?" Liv whispered quickly.

Rachel shrugged. "Don't see why not," she said after a couple of seconds' thought.

Alex sat down next to me. "We were worried about you," he said to Rachel.

"It was stupid of me," she replied. "I got lost on the way to the bathroom."

I wondered how Alex was going to react when we found out where Rachel had been. I half expected him to get all weird because Rachel had discovered some secret inner sanctum of the castle and now he was going to have to lock us all up. Alex made a face after Rachel finished recounting her tale for him.

"In the labyrinth? Wow. It's supposed to be locked off, like, forever. I'm surprised you got out. I used to try and mess around in there when I was kid. They were always having to come in and get me and I used to hide in the dark. It's crazy. How did you escape? There's only one way in and out."

"Someone heard me trying the doors and let me out. A servant I think, a scary looking woman if you don't mind me saying so."

Alex laughed and shrugged. "I'm not sure who you saw," he said to Rachel.

"Not the ghost?" I asked.

Alex shook his head. "Not unless she's started talking. The maid ghost is very young anyway. She was only nineteen when she died."

Alex looked at his watch.

"I have to be somewhere," he said. "See you tomorrow?"

We said goodnight and Alex left us spread out on the sofas. Rachel watched him go. "Wait a minute," she said, adding in a whisper. "Make sure he's gone."

Liv and I looked at her blankly and waited.

"It's something he said," she continued, "about there being one way in and one way out."

We waited for her to go on.

"Like I said, when the lady took me through the empty room we came out onto a landing, with a red carpet. But it was right over in that far corner, the opposite end of the wing to where I got in."

I frowned at her.

"What do you mean? That you came out diagonally across from here?"

Rachel nodded.

"I think I mean that Alex doesn't know about the spiral staircase. I went in one side, somewhere through that door," she pointed across the lounge, "and I ended up coming out over the other side of the castle. And another thing," she added quickly, "that woman was asking me how I got in, everything. She really interrogated me. I tried to look and sound as dumb as possible, as if I wasn't sure, and I acted all confused like I couldn't remember anything."

"But it can't be that you know more about the castle than Alex, just by making a mistake!" I laughed.

"Let's go look for ourselves," Liv said excitedly, her large blue eyes sparkling, "Come on!" She sprung up.

Rachel rose cautiously. "I'm not sure we should."

But Liv was heading for the door at the far end of the lounge and we hurried to catch up to her.

Once through the door we let Rachel go ahead of us. She opened the door to the right and we all went down the narrow corridor that she had told us about. There was a door at the end on the left. Rachel paused in front of it and then turned the handle. It was locked.

Ryan appeared at the top of the stairs as we came back from trying the door. Rachel told him everything quickly.

"You've been trying to see if you can get back in there, haven't you?" he asked accusingly, "We don't want to do anything stupid."

He glared at the three of us in the same way his father would.

Liv started to protest, but Ryan held his hands up. "Okay, look, let's get some fresh air, check on the boys and then make it an early night."

The atmosphere had become fraught with tension, and this was the best idea I had heard all day. We all needed to chill out.

I was thinking of the following day and hoped it would be less full of odd surprises than the one that was about to end. We said goodnight to Luce and the others in the stable yard and, amid a chorus of yawns, turned for the door in the wall and up to our rooms.

I awoke nice and early and was ready to spring out of bed and into my terrific bathroom. We had a relaxed time at the stables that morning with Hans, followed by a gentle ride out past the lake and the woods that lined the driveway. Hans was with us on Domino this time. Toby, the leader of our pack, was working with Mr. Vazquez and Benicio. Luce enjoyed the pace of the ride, and on our return we had to wait while they shot a scene with Benicio on Toby in front of the main entrance, with the stable archway in the background. It seemed to take forever, and eventually we were allowed back into the yard. Benicio had been ushered off as soon as the shot wrapped.

The day passed pleasantly, with chores around the stables and a leisurely check of the paddock fencing, then a water fight by the stream when we thought we were far enough away from the yard – that Red and Luce tried to join in. It was suddenly time to shower and change and head for the lounge to rest and wait for dinner.

Alex was back with us as we took up our usual position in the round of the turret. I saw him look at his watch and suddenly hoped he didn't have to be somewhere else. I didn't want to think that. I just did.

"Maybe we could all go for a walk or something," he suggested.

Alex led us on a tour of the immaculate lawns that fell away from the patio. We had a look at the outdoor pool on the middle tier. It was a huge blue rectangle, immaculate and inviting.

We ambled back up to the castle and down the gravel drive, now a familiar route past the main entrance and on to the stables. It was nice being in a group, chatting away, listening to Alex telling us fascinating stuff and asking questions. I felt very relaxed and happy.

"Hello," I heard Rachel say in a strange voice.

I looked up. We were all in the middle of the yard looking at Benicio. He was standing at Red's door, with his hand tenderly placed on the Chestnut's nose.

"Hi!" he said. "I hope you don't mind…"

"Why should we," Ryan said, in an almost friendly tone.

"I like to be with them," he said. There wasn't one of Benicio's 'security' people in sight. Just him.

"Hi, Salma," he said. "Where's your black beauty?"

Panic shot through me. I rushed forwards, Ryan too, swearing. We flung ourselves against the half door and craned our heads into the stable. Luce was not there!

Chapter Five

Benicio was quickly there beside us and then we were all tearing around the corner toward the woods. Ryan skidded to a stop just ahead of me and ran back. "I'll get Red," he yelled.

Benicio and I kept on sprinting into the trees down the grass trail that veered away from the stables. My heart thumped in my chest as I ran and called for Luce. After what seemed like just a few seconds, I heard the pounding of hooves catching up to us. I turned and saw Ryan bareback on Red, followed by Alex on Domino, riding bareback too, and struggling to stay up. I slowed to a jog and saw Liv and Rachel running to catch up to us. Alex came alongside me and slithered to the ground before he fell. He pushed Domino forwards toward me.

"Take him," he shouted. "He'll be fine with you."

I looked at him, wide-eyed at the craziness of the suggestion as I grabbed hold of Domino's mane. I seriously doubted Alex's assertion but I needed a ride, now, and it was worth a try. I dove toward Domino as he began to slow and there wasn't a moment to worry about how he would react as I went for a running mount. It was a while since I'd done one, and I just made it onto his wonderfully broad back, gripping the mane tightly and rising to a gallop along the path after Ryan.

"Be careful!" Benicio yelled after me.

Domino was tense and I had to use all my skills to maintain control and to desperately try to reassure him that I was in charge. Riding him felt exactly like being bareback on Luce. They seemed to have identical width. There was the same strength in the limbs that I was used to. The most amazing difference though, was in the mane.

While Luce's was lush and thick, Domino's was sparse, as was typical of an Appaloosa, and there wasn't much to grab hold of. I felt him relax a little as the first clearing came into view through the dusk. Ryan had continued on along the main path, but I decided to take one of the smaller paths off the clearing to the left, heading, I thought, almost straight back to the castle. I called constantly for Luce and felt physically sick. We had to find him or I would go crazy.

As the trees flew past on either side I asked Domino to slow and his response was instantaneous. I felt the relief of knowing that I was in control of my new mount, despite the craziness of the chase. It suddenly struck me to question whether we were doing the right thing, racing around in the woods as the light faded.

Right in the depths of the forest it felt almost dark. I knew that if I was lost in the trees as the night took over I would be terrified. We slowed to a stop and then walked on. I listened, looking for sight of the castle walls ahead without luck. I was worried I was shooting off on the path away from the castle and heading diagonally into the depths of the forest.

Then a call reached my ears. I couldn't make it out but the second time I heard it.

"Got him!" It sounded like Benicio – to my left. As if by magic another path appeared leading off to the left so I steered Domino around onto it.

"Ryan, Salma! Come back! We've got him!" That was Liv.

Then Benicio again saying, "Come back!"

I cantered toward the voices, my heart leaping with a joy I can't describe, as it seemed they had found Luce.

The path was like a tunnel in the trees and I realized it ran parallel to the castle. I could just see the gray wall to my right, barely visible now as darkness took over.

At least, if I got lost now, I would be able to find my way back. I also realized that the path I had been on, before I heard the voices and turned off, was leading me into the heart of the woods as I had feared. Domino knew where he was going though, and after a few more yards I could pick out the figures of Alex, Rachel, Liv and Benicio at the entrance to the yard. The path was taking me right to the back of the stable block.

My heart surged as I saw Luce standing with the others, safe, with a head collar. Liv clasped the rope tightly. Luce spun toward me and whinnied as I dismounted. I buried my head in his mane and wiped away a tear of relief. Alex grabbed hold of Domino.

Then, just as I tuned into the strange expression on the three faces that greeted me, I saw that Luce had something tied around his middle.

"Boy is he glad to see you!" Alex said. I stared at the rope, which was tied around my horse. It was a thick climbing rope, the kind we have hanging in the school gym. The end of it trailed along the floor. Liv picked the end up and studied it. It wasn't frayed. It just looked like the end of a rope. The whole rope, including the trailing end and the part around Luce's girth, was about 10 yards long. I clutched at him as his sides heaved.

"Something weird is going on here," Liv said holding up the end as "exhibit A."

We heard the sound of hooves thundering out of the forest and turned to see, with even more relief, Ryan returning down the trail.

Ryan sighed heavily at the sight of us, this time out of exhaustion and elation.

"Luce came flying down that trail at us," Alex began the story. "He nearly took us all out. There was no sign of anyone else."

Luce's breathing had become more regular and he now stood quite calmly as I worked on the crude double knot that was securing the heavy rope. My fingers hurt by the time I'd managed to ease the difficult first knot free.

"We took off after him and Benicio grabbed for the rope, but he was slowing down anyway," Liv continued.

"Lucky for me," Benicio said, gingerly flexing his shoulders. "I would have lost my arms."

Ryan took the end of the rope from Liv and looked around the group.

"What on earth is going on here?!" he said, his voice high. "Let's get this off him."

Ryan helped me loosen the second knot. The rope was

so coarse that the friction between the fibers was keeping it tight.

I led Luce through to the stable yard slowly. We needed the lights to check him over properly. My heart was still pounding, thinking about why he'd been taken and the fact that he had raced through the forest with the rope lashing around his legs. Anything could have happened! Luce didn't seem at all lame. I was anxious about what we were going to find when we surveyed him under the lights. He was calm and stood obediently. He seemed to understand what we were doing, but he must have been so confused.

Ryan studied his legs diligently. I almost had to dare myself to look at his coat where the rope had been as Rachel passed me a body brush.

The others were all talking nonstop as they saw to the other two horses, voicing question after question. The harsh yard lights showed, amazingly, that there was almost no sign of where the rope had been tied, except for puckering marks in his coat, which I smoothed over easily. Despite my gentle work he made a little jump sideways as I went over the sides of his back. There was definitely some soreness, but Ryan and I were both confident that was all he had suffered. He had a bucket of water, and we would offer him some more at intervals until he had enough, and then stay with him until we were positive he was ready to settle into his stable.

I held his head tenderly and whispered to him, stroking his nose. He snorted softly and nuzzled my neck.

"I have to tell Dad," Ryan said. "About the guys on the moped too. Can you finish up here?"

I nodded and he walked to the door in the castle wall. Our week at the Castle was hanging in the balance.

With the others safely stabled, and eventually Luce, I joined everyone in the middle of the yard. Liv was clutching at the rope.

"It was tied to another rope," she said and pointed to a section near the end. "Look. Can you see the straggly blue fibers?"

She was right.

"Why on earth did someone need to do that?" Rachel asked. "Why would you take a horse and tie it up?"

"I don't think he was tied up." Benicio said quietly. I was still pinching myself that he was hanging out with us despite the craziness of the situation.

"What are you thinking?"

Benicio put his hand to his chin and shook his head. I'd seen him do the exact same gesture in a film. "I wish I could tell you."

I shook my head. "He's okay. That's the main thing."

Liv sighed. "Yeah. You're right."

"Shall we go and get a cola or something?" It was Benicio's suggestion. I liked the idea of sitting on the patio with him quietly, but I couldn't leave Luce just yet.

"Good idea," I told him. "I'll come in a minute." Liv nodded too. I looked at Alex and suddenly realized how quiet he'd been.

"Are you coming too?" I asked.

He smiled quickly, as if I'd jogged him out of a moment of deep thought.

"If that's okay," he replied, sounding nervous.

"It's your house," I said, smiling, "Of course it's okay."

66

Alex was worried. It was obvious to me, anyway. We'd come to his home – a visit that he'd been looking forward to for months – and some very odd and dangerous things were happening. And Ryan was right. We couldn't keep it from Mr. Vazquez any longer, even if it meant we were off the film.

"I'll be along in a minute." I told them.

The patio was bursting with members of the film crew. It was the place to be in the evenings. Benicio's bodyguards were at the table next to us, probably where they had been all evening. They nodded to him as he sat down at an empty table, and eyed us all suspiciously.

The Count and his wife were entertaining Jonathan the director and Steven. Alex's mother was smiling a lot and seemed to be enjoying herself, and the Count did too. They looked less odd sitting there chatting away. Alex's mom was the kind of person you just worried about on sight. She looked so fragile and quiet. Tonight though, there was a light in her eyes and her beautiful smile was the same as Alex's. Like him, she had a kind face.

Sandy was also there – surrounded by young men from the crew. She saw us and chose to ignore us. I got the feeling that relations between her and Benicio were a bit frosty. We had already shown her that we weren't impressed.

Benicio stayed with us, laughing with Rachel and Liv about the time they had first met on a film set, telling Alex and me the whole story. Liv and Benicio seemed to have settled into a nice flirty friendship. Ryan appeared and told us everything was okay. We were all thrilled to hear we weren't about to be carted home. I was looking forward to hearing the details later. Then Sandy appeared, slinking her arm around Ryan's waist. I felt my nose twisting. She ignored us all in fine style.

"Looks like I'm coming out with you guys for a ride tomorrow," she announced flicking her hair. "Steve thinks it's a rocking idea!"

Yeah, *whatever*! I looked at Liv and Rachel and their faces made me want to burst out laughing. I didn't want Sandy out with us on our horses either, but it seemed there wasn't anything we could do about it. I just knew it was going to be less than fun. And there was no way she was riding Luce. Absolutely no way.

The party broke up at ten. Everyone had an early start and the new schedule didn't seem to give anyone any time off. I was glad when my head hit the pillow only to be awakened by a light knock at the door a few minutes later.

Chapter Six

I turned the tiny bedside light back on and made an attempt to smooth my hair. It always gets ten times crazier when I'm in bed.

"Who is it?" I whispered.

"It's me."

I expected the girls might come in for a late night chat, but not Ryan.

"Come in," I called.

He had a baggy navy t-shirt on and black cut-off tracksuit bottoms with bare feet.

Ryan had nice feet – tanned looking like the rest of him. I pulled my knees up to my chest so he could sit down.

"Dad's down in the trailer," he told me.

"What did he say when you told him about tonight?"

Ryan shrugged. "He looked at me as if I was making it all up. We went back to the yard and checked Luce again. Dad thinks the same as us – a slight soreness from the rope like there was a weight on it, especially on his back where it might

69

have pulled and rubbed. It's nothing that a numnah and an easy day tomorrow won't cure."

It was a relief to hear this.

"Maybe he pulled someone along the ground as he escaped," I offered. "He must have escaped, right? I don't think whoever it was had finished with him, whatever crazy thing they were trying to do."

Ryan ran his hand through his curly hair, scraping it back from his face momentarily and nodded slowly.

"What else did your Dad say?"

"He was trying to figure it out like we are. I expected him to say we were packing up and going, but…" Ryan trailed off and let out a quiet little laugh. "It was like he would rather stay and find out what's going on. I could see his brain ticking. He asked where Luce was running from when they saw him coming back. He wanted to know all about the rope too. I think," Ryan paused, "I think he's gone off into the woods now to see what he can find."

"Well he's not scared of the dark, is he," I said, chuckling quietly.

I didn't worry about Mr. Vazquez wandering around in the woods at night. He could more than handle himself. The guy was *massive,* with the broadest shoulders I'd ever seen – stocky and incredibly strong, but he was quick and agile. He had to be for his work as a stunt man. If anyone was creeping around in the dark and up to no good they should be wishing that Mr. Vazquez didn't find them.

He would make sure that the horses were safe too. And I would have been down there if he wasn't, making sure no one touched a hair on Luce's mane. I think I would die to protect him. I had to try not to dwell on what had happened

70

earlier because the idea of someone taking my horse and tying a rope around him made me feel beyond mad.

"He'll make sure no one tries anything tonight," Ryan said. "He's probably setting up a network of lasers as we speak."

It was good that we could crack jokes now.

"They think it's the paparazzi, and the perimeter security has been increased," Ryan told me. "There will be a helicopter patrol too. And anyway, we can't just walk out on a contract like this if we can avoid it. It's our third big movie in a row now, and we need to keep the momentum up. If we bail out, someone will happily fill our shoes."

"What about Hans, does he know all about it?"

Ryan nodded.

"Dad told him tonight. They're probably both out there. They've been riding together and having a drink in the evenings. Hans had lived in Spain in the region where Dad's from. It's been ages since Dad has met anyone he can talk to about home. So, there're two of them making sure the horses are safe. I can guarantee you that nothing is going to happen again. There's no reason to leave now."

The way Ryan asserted this made me believe him. Everyone was on the case now and Mr. Vazquez was being cool about it. Nothing else was going to happen. I looked at Ryan sitting in the cozy room and everything felt okay again.

"If anyone messes with our boys again we'll find them," Ryan said firmly.

"Alex and everyone will help. And Benicio!" I added with a laugh.

Ryan's eyes were wide. "Yeah. What's going on there?"

"He's bored with his meathead security men, and he's grown up a bit."

71

"But why hang with us?"

I shrugged. "I don't know. He kind of knows us, but I suppose it's because we're relatively… real?"

Ryan nodded.

"Some big actors only hang out with other actors on location. Others stay in their trailers with their 'people' and there're a few who seem to actively seek out the crew and hang out with ordinary people – well, as ordinary as people can be on a film set anyway," he grinned.

I knew what he meant. We were in a totally unreal world. I'd felt it as soon as we arrived and saw everyone gathered on the patio.

I wondered if he was pleased that Sandy would be joining us for the ride the next day…

"Rachel said Alex told you some amazing story about his shifty uncle and the family jewels?"

I told Ryan Alex's tale about Uncle Philip and the maidservant, Sofia.

"I wonder where the jewels are hidden," I mused as I finished relaying the story.

"Try that labyrinth, for starters," Ryan replied. "I don't think I want to, though. Rach looked a little freaked out by it all."

"It was the woman who fished her out who was scary! I wish we could, you know, snoop around the place – just the corridors or whatever. Alex and Hans didn't say we couldn't explore, did they?"

Ryan made a face.

"No, but it's someone's home, remember."

He was right.

"But I wonder what the room is at the top of the labyrinth? If Rachel's right and there is a room there?"

"We can take a look tomorrow night if you want – see if we can find it." Ryan grinned and raised those super eyebrows at me.

"You just said…"

"I know," he cut in, gesturing with his hands to placate me. "Can't do any harm, though. There are about 100 people staying here as well as some crew in their trailer park. Don't you think people have snooped about a bit, as you said? I don't think any sections are closed off. Hans would have told us. I'll knock on your door at midnight."

"I'll be ready," I answered.

Ryan moved to go. Just then my door clicked and fell open with a creak. I looked at Ryan.

"Must not have shut it properly," he said and left.

I pulled the covers over myself and tried not to think about the young maid.

Mr. Vazquez reported at breakfast that there had been no sign of anyone snooping around the yard last night.

The plan was for us to go on a leisurely trail ride over to the location site. I couldn't wait to see Luce in the morning, and fortunately he was back to his old self, staring at me, snorting, stamping – his usual repertoire. I tacked him up gently using a numnah and he didn't move a muscle. Rachel got Velvet ready for Sandy. Rachel didn't seem to mind not riding as Steve had offered to take her for a spin in his sports car over to the location instead of riding with us.

Then there was Sandy, dressed to the nines, all brand new. She acknowledged Ryan and Mr. Vazquez who moved swiftly over to her. If mounting up was anything to go by we were in for a treat. Some people just don't do well with horses – and Sandy was one of those people. The third time she got lucky and, after much hair flicking, she was finally ready to go. Liv's face had tears running down it when I looked at her and I laughed into Luce's mane as we left the yard.

We rode out along the road we had come in on, following the long drive up to the ridge and over and down past the lake. Then we veered cross-country through some welcome open space. Alex was with us and led the way along the trail the length of a few fields, then through a nice thicket of trees and finally to the location.

It was a large field with a hedge at one end and the woods skirting two sides. Luce seemed very content. We were all taking it nice and slow for him. I figured he would be itching for a gallop. He was the last horse to be calm about anything anyway. He was tough and he had been through some hard times in his life before he came to us.

As we reached the edge of the field I saw the tracks laid ready for the moving camera. Luce sounded a triumphant whinny. He was ready too and I patted his neck, thrilled that he was fit and well.

We set up the start of the shot and then raced the length of the field, Ryan and Rachel slightly ahead simulating the race within a race that Benicio and Sandy's characters took part in. The other people riding in the shot weren't important to the film, so they could be just anyone, luckily for us! We'd have to come out here with Sandy and Benicio to do closer shots too and just be blurred figures in the background.

The scene was easy, but it was good to do a run-through

74

in the field, especially the last try after Rachel and Steve arrived and he gave us more technical information about where all the cameras would be and what they were trying to capture. We already knew the angles we would be shot from but it was great to have Steve's vision of the scene. He didn't want us to practice it too much either, so it would look like a spontaneous gallop in the film. It was all going to be great.

As I predicted, Sandy managed to be the only person ever to make our dependable Velvet look difficult. He turned and pranced in the field and had definitely had enough of his rider.

As we left, the replacement caterer's van arrived in the field. It looked like everything would be fine with the new schedule without any more delays.

Alex rode alongside me on the way back. His quiet, apprehensive mood of the evening before seemed to have gone.

"I've just asked Ray and the others if you'd all like a ride out this afternoon in the woods again. You'll come too, won't you?"

"Of course," I told him, "If that's what everyone wants to do I'm up for it."

My reply came out a bit wrong, like I'd only go for a ride if everyone was coming along. I was probably thinking about it too much. Alex didn't seem bothered by what I'd said and I started to look forward to the afternoon immediately. None of us would ever say no to another full day of riding and exploring.

Just then Velvet and Sandy went shooting by us with Ryan in hot pursuit. He managed to effortlessly grab Velvet's reins and took control of the situation. Sandy made some high-pitched noises and then jumped down from the saddle. She headed off down the bank and across the lawns toward the patio without a backwards glance. Ryan turned to look at us, trying to hide a grin.

"Apparently Velvet's 'evil'," he called back. It was the funniest thing I'd heard in a long time. From the sound of Liv's laughter, she agreed.

We were ready to go again three hours later – without Rachel, who was on set helping with Velvet. No one envied the afternoon she was in for with Sandy, who would no doubt refuse to go near our sweet bay stallion until the crew begged on their knees and she'd consulted with her agent.

We were due for a surprise as we stood mounted up in a huddle waiting for someone to lead us off. Through the archway came Mr. Vazquez and Benicio. Our new friend waved and we watched as Mr. Vazquez saddled Toby. Hans had been about to do the same and catch up to us so that Toby didn't miss out on the ride, but it seemed that there was a slightly different plan emerging.

Mr. Vazquez crossed the yard to where we all stood ready to go.

"He goes with you," he said. "He asked politely so I said 'yes' and he needs more work with Toby. They are nearly ready, but a good ride will be good for both of them."

We all nodded as Benicio walked Toby over to us. He looked strange in a riding hat, actually, more uncomfortable. He was fingering the strap like a beginner at his first lesson.

We set off out of the yard at the back corner by the paddock and began treading the now familiar wide path into the woods.

I hung back. I wanted Luce to see everyone ahead and feel really safe. Ryan and Red were right in front of us. If my horse was worried at the prospect of going back into this part of the woods, I wanted him to see his best friend right there in front of him. As we passed the point where the trees began, Luce snorted, but in his usual mischievous way. He seemed relaxed and I leaned forward and patted his neck. This ride would be the one that would tell me how his escapade the evening before had affected him. Ryan and I had chatted about how he might react, but I think we both knew that he would be okay.

Luce didn't seem to know "scared" these days. If he was frightened, he would act up and show signs of aggression. I think that was why he was so dear to me. He had been through bad times, but he was defiant. It was like nothing could crush his spirit. My horse was brave and wonderful.

Secretly, I was watching him for any clues about the night before. Luce knew where he had been and I felt him urging me forward while staying within the realms of behaving. He was eager to press on. I knew horses had incredible memories. I'd read about their homing abilities and how they spot landmarks they have seen before. I wanted him to show me where they had taken him.

Benicio looked over his shoulder and gestured for me to come alongside him. Of course, I didn't need a second invitation. I got a fleeting picture of my mom going on about how she would run off with George Clooney if he called and asked – "Without a second thought," she said. Of course, it would never happen, and that was why she had said it, but my Dad's face was a sight! Benicio was one of those "run offs" for girls like me, looking down from a million posters on bedroom walls.

Toby seemed very content with Benicio as his mount. He was Mr. Vazquez's most senior horse: a huge, gentle, dependable gray stallion. He was the leader of the Vazquez stallions. The others respected him and looked up to him. He was intimidating as a stunt horse because of his size and presence, but the most trouble he usually gave to a new mount on set was being a little irritable if his rider didn't show him who was boss. Toby expected them all to be as accomplished and directive as Mr. Vazquez or Ryan. He was used to getting clear aids and he didn't like passengers. He seemed to lose a little of his patience with weak riders.

"I still love this guy." Benicio told me. "I have my own horse at home just like him."

I grinned at him.

"After you visited us?"

Benicio nodded. "I know I acted like a jerk trying to buy Toby before I left. It was a way of being rude to Mr. Vazquez. But…" he held his finger up. "I fell in love with all your horses that week and I knew I wanted one of my own."

"What's your horse's name?" I asked him.

"Sunny. He's a gray too. I ride him every day when I'm home." He paused for a moment. "I was happy when I found out you would all be here – on this location – and so I can show my different side." Benicio glanced at me shyly.

I nodded at him. He really was ashamed of his show the summer before.

"You weren't that bad," I told him.

"I was," he replied.

"Okay you were, but we're glad to see you again and hang out and have a nice time." He laughed at me.

I hadn't told anyone what Benicio told me about his

mom getting ill and I wouldn't now. He seemed to have
picked me out. He was nice to everybody and I was starting
to think that he might actually see me as a friend. I didn't
think he liked me. I hoped not. He was only four years
older than I. I say 'only,' but it seemed like a lot, actually. I
was happy being his friend.

Up ahead, Alex gave a signal. Benicio gave me a challenging
look. "Great!" he said and then shot away from me down
the avenue. Luce didn't hesitate for more than a second and
then Ryan and Red were next to us, the Chestnut and Luce's
strides a perfect mirror of each other. We joined up again at
the center of the huge first clearing.

"If we take the right hand fork when we get to it and
follow the side trail all the way around we'll end up by the
lake," Alex told us. He nodded at me.

"Is he okay?"

"Totally," I replied. "He's loving it!"

Alex's kind eyes smiled back at me.

"Good," he said, "Let's go."

Everyone was smiling.

"Race you, Ben," Liv cried. She giggled and turned
Chokky into a sprint. Benicio was right behind her making
for the continuation of the main trail.

Alex followed, then Ryan and finally me. I knew I
shouldn't really have been bringing up the rear after what
had happened to Luce the day before, but I was confident
that he was okay. Luce was eager to press on again and rose
to a full gallop, plunging into the woods. I loved the feeling
of the trees flying by on either side, and the thud of the
hooves on the grass. We reached the second clearing, a few

seconds after Ryan. He turned to look back and make sure I was following.

We had almost reached the center of the space when I felt Luce pulling to the left. I urged him straight initially, but he persisted, so I let him turn and lead me where he wanted to go. We still had plenty of time to turn and he did so gracefully, well before the edge of the clearing. Luce cantered on, following the contour of the trees, and circled around the edge of the open space. I had no idea where he was heading – but then I saw it. He had picked out a narrow path about a hundred yards around the perimeter of the clearing from where we were supposed to have continued along the main path.

We had to slow down to negotiate the narrow entrance to the path and then we once more had the trees rushing by on either side of us. I was on Luce's magical mystery tour and I felt a fizz of excitement, then acute apprehension and then concern about finding the others again. I decided I would worry about that later. We were too far away to be able to see the castle and to get a bearing, but I figured that we were almost heading back toward it on the narrow grassy passage that my horse had discovered.

Luce had slowed to a determined canter again and we rode on for a minute; a minute that felt like a lifetime. There were no forks in the trail and no open spaces, just a very gentle curve to the right that meant I couldn't see back where I had come from or where Luce was leading me. He finally slowed, making a calm transition to a walk.

"Okay, boy?" I said. "Now what? Where are we going now?"

He had built up the drama brilliantly. I didn't much like it that we had slowed down. It made me apprehensive

and, after a few more seconds, fearful. I had felt fine with
the trees rushing past a couple of yards on either side,
and the thud of his hooves filling my ears, but now there
was a deathly quiet, and the sound of Luce's walk was
punctuating the air with tension.

I knew what it felt like to be underneath a canopy of
tall trees. We were surrounded by magnificent woods at
home and I was used to the atmosphere – a kind of silent
suspense. That was what I felt now, but it was tinged with
something else, something sinister.

I looked up to see the trees covering the sky above
the path. It was gloomy, and the knowledge that we were
totally alone consumed me. I swallowed and patted Luce's
neck, thinking how quickly my excitement at him taking
me somewhere new had become fear.

I patted his neck and swallowed again.

"You show me, mister."

A rustle in the undergrowth right next to the path made
me flinch. I clasped my hand to my mouth to stifle a cry.

Luce walked on as I took three deep breaths. I needed
to pull myself together for both our sakes. My horse had
brought me here and I couldn't fail him by panicking.

Then we stopped still. Luce didn't want to move and I
waited patiently, filling my head with thoughts of Ryan or
Alex – even Benicio appearing in front of me, smiling and
chastising me for losing the group.

The path ahead continued on, still curving gently
around to the right. On either side of me magnificent
lindens and copper beech trees stretched upwards, their
trunks like majestic Roman columns. Tall poplars filled
the spaces in between, and here too were silver birches.

There was something ghostly about the white birch trunks. I pushed away the image that they brought of bright white skeletons waiting for me in the forest and asked myself who I would prefer to be my knight in shining armor. It was Ryan's face that appeared in my mind's eye, but then Alex replaced him.

I leaned forward and placed my hand on Luce's neck. He began to paw the ground. I realized how different this action was from his usual stamping. The aggression in his feet was frightening, even to me. His head was down, every mannerism showing he was prepared to attack.

"It's okay," I told him, "Show me where you want to go."

So he walked on. I realized I'd been holding my breath and let it out slowly. The relief at moving forward again was immense. We continued around the curve of the path and there, five yards ahead, was a wide-open space. Luce stopped again exactly as the path opened into the clearing. It was much smaller than the other ones in the main ring, and circled by really tall poplar trees growing very close together, making it feel like the inside of a stockade. There was something else that was different about this clearing and it took me a moment to realize it. The trees were all covered in a choking ivy that crept up almost to the top, and it was all over the floor of the forest too, eating up everything in its path and smothering the life out of it. Luce again stamped the ground fiercely and then reared. Subconsciously, I think I must have been ready for it and my ears were split by his full-bloodied shriek. My heart felt as if it would pop out of my chest as his front quarters touched down. I waited for a repeat

and then urged him forwards. It was time to take control now. He complied and we walked toward the center of the clearing. I expected something to come and whisk us away to a parallel universe after the tension Luce had just piled onto me.

We weren't whisked away, though. I looked around the odd open space and scanned for a path leading out the other side. I was relieved to see it directly across from where we were.

We paused in the center for a moment as Luce pawed the ground and whinnied. He really couldn't have told me any more clearly. This was where he had been. But why? And what about the rope?

Once again my mind began to whirr with questions. Luce decided he'd had enough and we were off across the clearing. I was praying that somehow, from deep in the woods, we'd get to the lake and find the others.

Chapter Seven

"Did you get lost?" Liv asked, laughing. "We were just about to send out a search party."

It was a relief to see the group of smiling faces greeting me by the water.

"How long have you been here?"

"Ages!" Liv cried.

"Liars!" I grinned back. I really had no idea how long Luce and I had played out our latest drama.

Ryan was smiling cautiously. "Is he okay? We realized you weren't right behind us so we thought you'd be taking it slowly. We were just starting to get a little bit worried."

"He's fine." I told Ryan. "He took me somewhere weird."

They all frowned and I explained exactly where we had ended up after we had left the main trail. Luce had joined the others in taking a drink from the little stream and we all sat sprawled out next to the lake on a grassy bank. Mostly, I addressed my story to Alex. He nodded when I explained how I got to the clearing.

"That's right in the center," he told us. "It's a really

strange spot, difficult to figure out why that clearing's there really." He made a face. "Just that narrow trail leading in and then out. I don't like it there very much. It's too quiet – a bit eerie, I think is the best description. Seriously, Salma, it's really right in the middle of the deepest part of the woods."

"It felt like it too," I told him.

"Were you scared?" Liv asked.

"It was a little scary," I replied. "It was mostly that it was so quiet, like Alex said – and gloomy with the trees covering overhead on the way in, where Luce stalled on me."

"He probably just did that to freak you out," Ryan said. We all laughed.

"It was like, he wasn't sure about going back there." I mused. "It's where whoever took him when he went missing. I'm sure of it."

"But what is there?" Benicio wondered aloud. "He did not show you anything more?"

"There was nothing to show," I told him, "Just the clearing, unless I missed something. He stopped in the middle, though."

Benicio looked at me like he was thinking hard.

We lounged in the warm sun next to the crystal clear water for a long time. I glanced over at the horses standing on a sandy area next to the stream. They looked relaxed and dreamy, their heads lowered and eyes partly closed. Luce and Red were resting on hind feet.

The next thing I knew, something soft and bristly was nuzzling my ear. I awoke to find Luce's muzzle about two inches above my head, and then the sound of everyone laughing.

We walked back slowly and approached the stables from the main drive. I wondered how the shoot had gone, first with Velvet and then over on the other side of the castle with the south wing as a backdrop. All the trailers were parked over there and it was the hub of the shoot each day. As we passed the entrance through to the center courtyard we heard a distant cheer and this made us all look at each other and smile. Shooting was wrapped for the day.

I fastened the bolt on Luce's door and he kicked it immediately, truly back to his old naughty self. I stroked his nose and told him he was silly and bad. He nibbled at the top of my shoulder, making me giggle. We had found Rachel in the yard when we returned and she reported that the scenes with Sandy on Velvet had gone well after a shaky start with Sandy asserting that Velvet "hated her." That made us all laugh. Then we told Rachel about my escapade in the forest.

Rachel stood on the other side of Luce's head and he stood quietly for once outside his stable. My horse promptly started on her neck. Rachel's head flew backwards and she let out her usual hysterical giggle.

Luce turned to me and nuzzled into the side of my face. "And now you want love," I said into his ear mockingly. "How a naughty stallion like you could ever be a stunt horse I have no idea." I stroked his silky nose again and looked across at Rachel.

She wasn't looking at me. She was staring up at the castle wall.

"What?"

Rachel kept on gazing up at the towering north wing. I looked too, quickly scanning the masses of windows as Luce pushed at my back.

"I just saw that woman," Rachel said. "The one who got me out of the labyrinth."

I turned to her, frowning. "At the window?"

Rachel nodded. "She was watching us."

There was apprehension in her voice and expression.

"You sure it was the same woman?"

"Definitely," she replied. "You wouldn't forget that face and even if I wasn't sure at first, the way she was looking at us convinced me. She moved away as soon as I saw her. There's something strange about her."

I glanced across the yard at Alex. He was frowning too and came over.

"Were you looking at that strange woman at the window?"

Rachel nodded. "She was the one I told you about, who got me out of the labyrinth. She was watching us. Do you know who she is?"

I felt a little shiver.

"It wasn't the ghost maid, was it?"

Alex shook his head.

"She's more of a presence. No. I've never seen that woman before in my life."

I had really started to look forward to being in my cozy room at the end of the long day. I was always tired by the time I got into bed but I'd been leaving the light on for about ten minutes and thinking about the day that had just gone by. This evening I was thinking about Alex before I turned the light off and in the moments before I nodded off. Always mixed in, though, were thoughts of the maid, and that she was around, watching.

I had just woken up again before the knock came at the door. I switched the light on, swung my legs out of the bed, and pulled on my tracksuit bottoms and baggy sweatshirt, which were lying on the nearby chair.

I called to Ryan to come in – saying a quick prayer that it *was* him and not some ghostly phantom messing with my door. Ryan closed the door behind him quietly and turned to me with a smile.

"Thought you might not answer." He was wearing black jeans and a black t-shirt. "I'd probably have left you to sleep. I figured everyone's really tired after today."

I laced up my sneakers and looked at my watch. It was 12:15 a.m.

"Let's go," I said.

Ryan opened the door again and I felt a bubble of anticipation at the thought of creeping around the castle in the dark – and that I'd be creeping around in the dark with Ryan. As we tiptoed across the hallway of our little apartment I tried to stop thinking about boys. It was starting to mess with my head.

We closed the door out into the corridor quietly and stood at the top of the narrow flight of stairs. Ryan whispered to me.

"There will probably still be people up and about, so we'll just look like we're on our way back to our rooms if we see anyone. No one will know we're not where we're supposed to be."

I nodded, thinking *except Hans and Alex… and Mr. Vazquez.* We descended our narrow stairs and two more flights, following the red carpet out to a landing. We were on the second floor now. Ryan stood next to me by the window and we looked down at the tidy square below. The wall lamps cast a gentle light over the flagstones.

I looked over to the south wing. If Rachel was right, the room at the top of the labyrinth was on the fourth floor, the last floor before the roof started. It made sense that the room would be in the middle of the fourth floor. Suddenly, I wasn't even sure why we were trying to find it, or even if it actually existed. We hadn't seen what Rachel had described to us for ourselves – secret rooms and hidden staircases. It was all the stuff of storybook adventures. Were we creeping around in the dark in a castle because it was the closest we were going to get to being one of the characters in one of those adventure books? Probably.

I gazed across the courtyard and up to the fourth floor. There were fifteen windows facing the courtyard on the fourth floor of the south wing. Now that I was studying this façade it was obvious that the three windows in the center of the row were different from the ones on either side of them. They jutted out slightly from the wall and they had crisscross leading detail across the glass.

"See those three windows," I pointed to them, "I think that's where we should go – whatever that room is."

"Okay," Ryan said in a low voice. "It's back up another two floors."

Something made me want to go back to my little room and my bed. I looked down at the courtyard. There were lights on all over the the castle: opposite, where the main entrance was, and the east wing where we were standing too. But where we were heading, the whole south wing of the castle was dark. There was not a single light on. That was what made me want to go back. If we wanted to go on a ghost hunt, we were going about it the right way.

Ryan led the way through the landing. I followed him to the large oak door. Through it was a corridor leading on, with the windows on our left and doors to the right – more rooms, probably guest bedrooms. It felt like I was on a train and passing people's compartments.

Eventually, we emerged at another landing. A wide staircase faced us. Ryan looked at me and we crossed the landing and ascended the stairs. They switched back in two flights and took us out onto an identical landing with more sofas and tables. After a short pause we carried on up the next set of stairs.

I knew there were people still up and about, but so far we hadn't come across anybody.

The fourth floor landing that we came out onto next was completely dark. Ryan and I crossed over to the window. We were facing the archway next to the main entrance, now far below us.

Ryan looked at me and gestured over his shoulder. "This way," he whispered. We moved away from the corner toward a door that would take us into the south wing for the first time.

That was when we heard another door open around the corner of the landing.

Ryan and I stared at each other in panic and our plan went straight out the window. He took hold of my arm and suddenly we were sitting down on the sofa under the window. Ryan leaned toward me and placed his hand behind my head and kissed me.

Whoever had come out onto the landing had walked past us, and seeming to sense our presence despite the lack of light, paused for a moment and then continued on across to the stairs and down.

I waited a short moment and we broke apart, without a word. We stood up and walked to the door we had been heading for.

"What happened to 'just look like we're going to our

rooms if we see anyone,'" I asked in another whisper.

Ryan didn't turn around.

"I don't know," he replied.

We headed into the South wing, the courtyard windows always to our left. I started to count them and check them off in my head. There were two out on the landing and through the door was what looked like a drawing room, but like the landing it was dark. There were two more windows. Here, there was moonlight. It was pale and ghostly and the elegant period pieces of furniture cast strange shadows across the floor. Ryan and I shuffled into the room and closed the door behind us.

There was something else about the room that was odd. I should have realized what it was right away but it took a moment. The carpet wasn't red. It was a pale color, and that said to me we shouldn't be here. We had entered somewhere private. There was no door opposite for us to head for, either.

We stood, almost huddled by the door, staring at the room. I felt that this was the point where we should turn back, but Ryan was undeterred.

"Where next?" he whispered.

The door at the diagonal corner seemed to be calling us. I pointed over to it and raised my eyebrows. Ryan nodded and we weaved our way through the moonlit room to the door. Ryan squeezed the handle down carefully and the large paneled door opened toward us. I half expected to be confronted by the sound of someone snoring and seeing the Count tucked in bed wearing one of those silly old fashioned white night caps. Instead, we found a strange L-shaped lobby. The only light source was from the courtyard window, which was now around the corner. We crept toward it. This was window number five. I began to worry. If someone found us here, our excuse of being on our way to our rooms would seem pretty lame. We were not supposed to be here at all. We'd have to act very dumb to convince anyone that we had gotten this badly lost!

I was the one who reached for the handle and slowly pushed open the door into the next room. It was a music room with a classic grand piano in the corner and beautiful wooden upholstered chairs. I counted the sixth courtyard window allowing the moonlight to flood the room. Opposite us was a door, and behind it had to be the room we were looking for. Ryan and I stood together staring across at the door. We exchanged an apprehensive glance and crossed the room. I clasped the handle, pulled it down slowly and leaned against the panel.

Locked. I pushed again just to be sure and turned to Ryan.

He was waiting for me to look at him, and in one hand he held up a key. The adrenaline was truly pumping and I felt like laughing hysterically at the sight of Ryan holding up the key with a glint in his eye. It was like we were in a video game and we had just gotten the ultimate "cheat."

"Where did you get that?" I hissed.

"Window sill," he replied, and carefully inserted the key into the lock.

I could feel a mix of hysteria and panic bubbling beneath the surface. Ryan seemed fearless, but he must have felt it too. He turned the key and the lock snapped neatly back.

Chapter Eight

We shuffled forward as the door opened. The room was a vast library, stretching back into the depths of the south wing. The walls were bookcases from floor to ceiling. Down the sides more shelves jutted out a short way at intervals. There was a large desk in front of the middle courtyard window and two reading tables in the center of the room. The floor was covered in large red Persian rugs. At the far end of the room was a suite of three sofas in patterned fabric. Once again, I felt as if I had stepped onto a movie set.

I heard Ryan murmur into my ear and I whispered back to him.

"It's amazing."

We wandered over toward the sofas. It felt safer being deep in the room, probably because we would be able to hide easily. I craned my neck around to take in the hidden corners of the library. The moonlight was still doing a good job of showing us everything.

Ryan was perusing the shelves.

"Imagine if we got locked in," he said. "We wouldn't get bored for about fifty years!"

It became darker as we moved into the depths of the room, but the moonlight reached almost back to where the sofas were set out.

I sat down on one of them and cast my eyes over the sandstone fireplace in the center of the back wall. This was the perfect place to curl up with a book in front of an open fire. I breathed in the scent of leather book jackets and old pages that the shelves held and laid my head back on the plump, rounded back of the sofa.

Ryan hadn't emerged from one of the vestibules between the shelves. I gave a whispered shout of his name but he didn't reply, so I sighed and rested my head back on to the sofa. If anyone entered the room now I was content in the knowledge that I was well hidden, and Ryan probably was too.

But then the door did open. I felt a bolt of terror and hunched down behind the arm of the sofa, drawing my legs up to my chest. My heart pounded and I wondered in a panic how Ryan was going to disguise himself as a shelf full of books. I had caught a flash of the figure before I ducked my head down, but it was impossible to make out who it was. It could have been anyone. Since Ryan and I had spontaneously hidden ourselves, it would be very bad news if we were discovered. We would look like the worst, creeping snoops. I breathed out slowly through my nose and heard it make a whistling sound. Just my luck, so I started to breathe through my mouth.

The footsteps started across the wooden floor, heading into the room and seeming to stop at the reading tables. The steps were slow, cautious maybe? Then no sound for what seemed like an eternity. I needed to move. One of my ankles was trapped awkwardly under my other leg and pins and needles were beginning to set in. My neck was bent against the arm of the sofa and was already starting to ache. It was so ridiculous I wanted to laugh. Then I heard Ryan's voice.

"Benicio."

The noise that followed sounded like someone jumping up to the ceiling and crashing down onto the reading tables. I popped my head up and saw Benicio falling sideways as the rug slid away with one of his feet. Ryan emerged from between some shelves and Benicio dragged himself back up. I stretched out my dead leg and stood up. As I put my weight on it my ankle buckled and I hit the floor. Benicio and Ryan's heads snapped around to look at me.

I got up and we all stared at each other for two to three seconds before we all started laughing. Ryan leaned onto the reading table for support, shaking and holding his stomach. Benicio crouched down on the floor. Just when I thought we might stop I let out a hissing giggle and that set us all off again. Ryan had managed to reach Benicio and ask him if he was okay.

"What are you doing here?" Benicio asked and then laughed again. I wiped my eyes as Ryan answered him.

"We could ask you the same thing."

Benicio shrugged and grinned.

"Just looking around," he said eventually. "I nearly died when you said my name, Ryan."

"Sorry," Ryan replied, trying to keep a straight face.

Ryan told Benicio all about the labyrinth and why we were creeping around. The mesmerizing effect of being in the library had made me forget that we were actually in the room we had set out to look for.

Ryan held his finger up and wagged it in the air. "It's good that you came in like that and scared us, Benicio," he said and let out a quiet laugh. "Because I ducked down in that corner and smashed my head on… this." Ryan turned on his heel and pulled out an office box file from the second shelf of the facing bookcase. On the spine was a label marked **Clippings – 1976** in black marker.

"What's odd is that it was jutting out, like it hadn't been put back properly."

Ryan opened the file as Benicio and I rounded the table to stand next to him and peer into the box at the aged newspaper cuttings. They were a mess.

"Don't know about you," I said. "But it looks as if someone has looked through these very recently."

The cuttings were in a few languages. The first three we couldn't understand, as they were in French, but they all carried the same two photos. One was of a young man, in a classic portrait shot. He was like a good-looking version of the Count, slimmer in the face and with a full head of hair. The second picture was of a lady, her head circled in a group photograph. Her hair was pulled back tightly off her face, thin and pretty. It was Sofia, the maid. The fourth cutting Ryan had out had the headline:

Disinherited son and maid raid family fortune.

We all leaned in, heads together. Ryan reached for the desk switch.

"Just for a minute," he said.

The yellow reading lamp illuminated the cuttings.

Ryan blew out a stream of air.

"Fugitives for 30 years," he said. "Where do you think they went?"

"It's like the plot of a movie," Benicio said. "Cool," he added slowly.

"We could be just feet from the jewels," I said excitedly.

"They must have turned the place upside down looking for them," Ryan said. "I'd start with that maze Rachel found."

"The one on the other side of that wall." Benicio pointed over to where the fireplace was. He knew the whole story of Rachel getting lost.

Ryan flicked the reading lamp off and the three of us drifted toward the back wall.

"It would just be too amazing if there was a secret switch," I whispered. "Shall we try and find one?"

Benicio nodded. "Why build the whole maze and the balcony around this room if you can't go between them, huh?"

"I think we should quit while we're ahead," that was Ryan. I turned to him in dismay.

"We'd be here all night, pushing and pulling at the books, he continued. "There are about three thousand on these back shelves alone and we have to be up in six hours."

Of course, he was right.

"But we can come back, yes?" Benicio said. "Just us three."

We nodded, Ryan more cautiously than I. He had his sensible hat back on.

We left the room quietly and retraced our steps back to the L-shaped corner landing overlooking the courtyard.

Ryan and I said goodnight to Benicio on the floor below. I said goodnight to Ryan and went into my room. Our kiss on the sofa seemed like hours before. Remembering it made me feel confused again. I fell asleep wondering if Ryan was just trying to keep me interested – and if I was being harsh to even think that way. And what about bags of hidden jewels? And did I really like Alex…?

Today was our last free day before the main shoot. I felt tired and bleary eyed at breakfast and was glad that in the end we hadn't tried to find a secret switch in the library shelves. I had gone through the motions at the stables later, feeling half asleep. Luce's attention-seeking ploys helped to focus my mind. He watched me as he toyed with the water bucket, threatening to tip it but just avoiding doing so. He eyed me constantly. I swear he knew that I was feeling slightly groggy.

Mr. Vazquez and Hans left the breakfast table, and Alex immediately took one of the vacant seats.

We all smiled at him and said hello. He smiled around the table but ignored me. It was obvious too. My hawk-eyed girlfriends each shot me a direct quizzical look. I felt like banging my head down onto the table and screaming, "Now what?!!"

"Rachel, what did that woman say to you? The one you saw in the labyrinth?"

I couldn't see Alex's face because he was turned away from me, probably deliberately, but it sounded like there was a real purpose to his question.

Rachel repeated exactly what she had told us.

"She mainly fired all those questions at me. Why?"

She played with her ponytail, as she always did when she was thoughtful.

"If I get the keys later, will you try and show me where you were when she found you?"

Rachel frowned and shrugged.

"Sure," she smiled.

"Can I come too?" Liv asked eagerly.

"Yes," Alex told her.

I wanted to join the party, but something stopped me from asking. It seemed Benicio, Ryan and I weren't the only detectives in the castle. Alex was trying to work something out. I wanted to ask him all about it so I tried one last time.

"What's made you curious about that woman, Alex?"

He turned to me and was about to speak, but then he looked away again and addressed the whole table. He obviously wasn't going to be overtly rude to me, but something between us had changed and it wasn't on my part.

"We had a theft, before everyone arrived, from the library."

I felt my cheeks go all hot at the mention of the library and prayed no one would notice. I glanced slyly at Ryan and he was staring down at the table.

"It was a plan of the castle. We might not have noticed because my father keeps them locked up and never lets anyone touch them. Not even me. But he had just catalogued them all so he knew exactly what was there, and he knew someone had used the key – don't ask me how he knew, but he did. The plan that was stolen was of the basement and the tunnels."

"Tunnels!" Liv almost screamed the word.

"There are tunnels under the castle linking up all the basements. There are supposed to be more leading out of the castle itself, but I think that's all a silly old myth."

Alex continued. "I just wondered if that strange lady had anything to do with anything odd like that, since I've never seen her before. I've spent the last day checking who exactly is here on the film and what their names are, against their photographs on the ID list." He looked at Rachel, "So if you and Liv meet me later and show me where you went in the labyrinth I can try and learn more about who on earth this woman is."

"A photographer," Ryan said. "Has to be. Benicio told us how much on-set pictures are worth of him, and if they sneak one of him and Sandy from a scene in the film, like a kissing scene, and try and make out like it's real, that's worth about a million dollars."

I felt myself turning tomato-colored for the second time in five minutes with Ryan's mention of kissing.

The others were all looking around and nodding their heads slowly. It all made sense now – someone hiding out posing as a member of the staff, and possibly someone else planning an escape route, using one of our horses, maybe. Or was it their way in? I remembered what Benicio said, "Photographers will do absolutely anything to get an amazing exclusive shot. They don't worry about breaking the law, anything is allowed. It is a sport to them." It really did all make sense.

But what about our visit to that clearing? Where did that fit into the grand scheme of things?

I started thinking about the schedule for the day ahead and whether we had any free time.

Mr. Vazquez was busy all morning with Benicio, Sandy, Toby and Velvet. They were shooting scenes where Benicio and Sandy's characters talk to each other as they are mounting up for their ride out. The film was all about a romance between the two characters – an adaptation of a famous book. The characters are all rich and meet up in beautiful locations all over the world. The castle and our bit of the film was all about their first meeting at a summer party.

We were going to take a look at the morning scenes being shot, and then after lunch we were all free. I heard Rachel saying that she would meet Alex at 2:30 in the upstairs lounge.

"Anyone want to ride this afternoon?" Ryan asked.

"Yes," I replied quickly. Alex, Rachel and Liv could do what they liked. I wanted to go for a ride, and maybe it would be another chance to check out the clearing with Luce. Although I'd been almost terrified when he took me there the first time, it had also been really exciting – just he and I on our own adventure.

Liv and Rachel were chatting about watching the shoot, and as I looked up I caught Alex's gaze flick away. So, something was definitely up and I couldn't even begin to figure out what I was supposed to have done wrong.

I was still racking my brain as we walked down the patio and rounded the farthest corner to the south wing of the castle. There was an explosion of activity as I looked up. The area surrounding another patio was alive with people. It seemed the whole crew was set up here, and we weaved our way through everyone to the front. I wasn't sure if we were supposed to, but Ryan led the way and I followed.

Benicio, Sandy and our two horses were standing in the middle of the space in front of the south wing's beautiful porch.

It was strange to see the two actors clasping the bridles of our horses as if they were their own. They stood close together while Steve seemed to be in discussion with the director, Jonathan, behind the cameras. Benicio was looking in one direction and Sandy in the other. It was obvious they didn't like each other at all. Sandy's beautiful hair was blowing gently in the wind as they waited beside our ever-patient pair. Velvet and Toby looked like they were posing for a portrait. Neither moved a muscle. I was so proud of them, still and calm while being surrounded by so many busy people and oddly shaped equipment.

"Look at them," Ryan whispered in my ear. "They haven't put a foot down wrong since we got here."

I nodded, and hoped tomorrow would work out the same for our shoot. We stood and watched for five takes until Jonathan was happy he had gotten what he was after, which seemed to be Sandy leading her horse along and gazing lovingly ahead at Benicio, who was leading Toby along slightly in front of her.

Then it was makeup and lighting adjustments – and more fussing for what seemed like forever. I couldn't believe the amount of lighting involved, considering it was a bright sunny day. Steve's discussions with various members of the crew between takes took forever too, and Jonathan would walk the actors through a slightly different way of doing the scene two or three times before he went back behind the camera – then Benicio had another suggestion which they tried out. I didn't know how everyone found the patience. I began to realize why some stars demanded luxury trailers to hide out in when they weren't needed – and why shooting a movie took three months for two hours' worth of film.

"You could never be an actress," Ryan said, like he had read my mind. His tone was deliberately intended to wind me up. "You haven't got the patience."

"I can be patient if I have to be," I protested. Ryan laughed and I felt slighted at his implied criticism. I was more impatient in my head than in practice. I'd never have learned to ride properly if I was truly impatient – and as for stunt riding, impatient people need not apply. I turned to him as a hush fell over the large huddle we were in.

"Do you really think I'm impatient?" I whispered.

He waited for a moment before he shook his head. Relief came over me. I knew at that moment I was crazy about him.

We watched the shoot some more and I worked out how the scene fit in with our big galloping scene. Benicio's last line as he mounted up was, "We'll have to hurry to catch the others." We were "the others." Us. How cool was that?! Obviously Benicio (David) and Sandy (Ella) would be continuing their flirtation during the little mounted race. We were just the background that didn't matter, but who cared!

"Hel-lo! Is anybody there?" Ryan had his head cocked toward me and he made a knocking gesture at the top of my forehead. I closed my eyes and shook my head, laughing.

"Miles away," I said, "thinking about tomorrow."

Ryan gestured over his shoulder.

"Come on. Let's go and see the boys."

We weaved our way out of the black T-shirted crew. My heart performed a little leap as I noticed Alex standing on the patio. Again, his eyes flicked away from me to Ryan.

"They've nearly finished for this morning," Ryan said cheerfully.

Alex nodded and kind of smiled, his posture not inviting us to stop and chat so we walked on.

"He's gone weird," Ryan said as we rounded the corner of the castle. I shrugged. I didn't want to tell him that I thought it was something to do with me.

"He seems to be on some kind of a mission about that woman Rachel saw, too," Ryan went on.

"Maybe he's worried the photographer is going to mess up the shoot, or that the Count's going to be blamed for them getting in?"

Ryan shook his head.

"It's not their job to ensure the security of the castle. The security contractors are responsible for that. If anything, the Count could complain that they haven't been doing their job properly."

"But if there are tunnels the Count hasn't told the security firm about then it's hardly their fault, is it?"

"Not really," Ryan replied, as we passed the umbrellas and patio furniture, "but Alex is definitely bothered about something. He's gotten all quiet and moody. I hope he snaps out of it soon because I thought he was cool."

I nodded. "I did too."

Ryan looked at me a bit too quickly. "Do you like him?"

I looked at him. Ryan never asked questions like that.

I waited a moment. "I don't think so," I laughed. The way it came out was like I wasn't sure. Not exactly what

105

I intended! We rounded the corner and crunched onto the gravel drive heading for the stables.

The uncomfortable moment was forgotten when we got to the field and saw Luce and Red playing an energetic game of "follow the leader," taking turns cantering after one another. It really did look like they had made up some rules and were having a whale of a good time. Chokky was ignoring them and drinking from the stream, no doubt hoping Velvet would be back soon. Our boys were making the most of the fact that Toby was absent. They always messed around more when he wasn't there.

"Fools!" Ryan said. Luce's ears flicked around at the sound and both Luce and Red headed over side by side. Red's chestnut coat was as luminous as the hazy sun and Luce's was shining like fresh glossy paint. We made a big fuss over them and promised we'd be back after lunch to take them out. Back in the yard Benicio emerged through the archway leading Toby, followed by Liv and Rachel with Velvet. He smiled broadly when he saw us.

"I love this guy," he said, patting Toby's neck. "If I had nothing to do I would spend all day with him." I loved hearing him say that. It just summed up what it was like to love horses.

"Was he good for you?" Ryan asked.

"Perfect." Benicio replied. "I think that he is near to deciding that I am worthy of him."

Toby let out a massive snort at that moment and we all giggled. It looked so nice seeing Benicio holding the reins so possessively. I thought he was right about Toby, our majestic gray leader of the pack. He seemed at ease with Benicio's ever increasing authority in his presence. For

Toby, as well as all of us, Benicio was someone we were starting to really respect.

"Is anyone riding this afternoon?" he asked.

Ryan replied, "Yes," and then added, "Before the hard work begins tomorrow."

"Can I join you? I'm not needed, and… Well, I just want to ride," Benicio laughed.

"Sure," Ryan told him. "We're setting off after lunch. We'll meet you here."

Lunch was fun. Not! Liv was in a bad mood because Ryan insisted we wouldn't wait until Liv and Rachel had finished with Alex before we went on our ride. She delivered acidic retorts to everything he said, until Mr. Vazquez decided he'd had enough and told her to be quiet. Then Alex joined us for dessert and very obviously ignored a direct question from me – which felt very embarrassing. After he left Mr. Vazquez asked Rachel and Liv to meet him at two o'clock to help with the afternoon scenes. Rachel smiled awkwardly and explained that they were meeting Alex, at his request. He looked at Ryan and me as if we should volunteer ourselves. I was desperate to go on the ride and Ryan obviously was too because Mr. Vazquez took one look at our faces and snapped.

"It's no resort camp here!"

I let out a laugh. I couldn't help it. It was his Spanish accent and maybe the stress of everything. He gave me the death stare, declared that he didn't need any of us, and rose from his seat.

As soon as his broad form disappeared from sight, Liv started laying into Ryan.

"Thanks for getting me into trouble..." etc., etc. I wondered if we were all starting to show the effects of being holed up together in the castle. We needed to smooth over the cracks and chill out.

"Maybe we'll all be in a better mood this evening." Ryan said, suddenly the voice of reason. There was silence. Liv didn't wait long, though.

"But you started it..."

Rachel's chair scraped backwards as she stood up. "I'm going to my room for a while, and then I'll meet you in the first floor lounge," she said to Liv, who eventually nodded.

"We'll do our detective work with Alex," Liv said, smiling back at her friend. "We'll tell you all about it later," she finished – with a sarcastic smile for Ryan – as if we were going to have to beg for a report.

He rose from the table. "Don't get lost in there and never find your way out," he said. Liv stuck out her tongue like a five-year-old and we all started laughing – even her.

"See you later," I said to the girls.

Benicio was waiting for us in the yard. I thought he would be. He really didn't seem to be able to get enough of being with the horses and hanging out in the yard. He already had Toby all tacked up. I loved it that he wanted to hang out with us.

"I got him from the field, no problem," he said, with pride. "He just came over when I went to the gate. He saw me and walked over from the other side of the field. So I get the head collar and take him here to get ready. It's okay, no?"

"Of course it is," I told him, as Ryan nodded. "You've been honored," he told Benicio. "No one can get Toby from the field if he doesn't like you."

We fell into line as the trees loomed ahead again and slowed to a walk just long enough to decide to head all the way through around to the lake as we had done the day before. Luce was loving it as we ploughed through the forest. At one point I spotted Ryan racing through the trees on a parallel trail as the pathways took us around the castle in a wide arc. Wherever there was a choice of trails, I let Luce decide which one to take. He always knew where he wanted to go and I realized he was taking the exact route that we had taken on the way back from the lake last time. I wondered whether he was able to work this out in his head and do the journey backwards. It would be difficult for a human to work out, but I knew that horses specialized in navigation. I wasn't sure whether they could work out how to do journeys back to front. I couldn't put anything past Luce, though. He was as sharp as a tack.

Ryan arrived at the lake first. He stood next to Red with a, "what took you so long?" look, but I could tell he'd only just dismounted. Benicio emerged from the trees half a minute behind me with a look of pure delight and exhilaration on his face. He brought Toby to a halt straight from the riding manual and joined us. We led the horses to the edge of the water and flopped down on the mossy bank. It was pleasant to feel the intense sun after the cool, damp air of the forest.

"Can you take us where you were yesterday, with him?" Benicio gestured to Luce, who was enjoying a long drink.

"I'd love to," I replied. "If I can find it." I looked at Ryan. "We've got time, haven't we?"

"I want to see it for myself too," he replied. He looked at

Benicio. "Do you know all the photographers?" he asked. "I mean, would you recognize a face if they were hiding as one of the crew or castle staff?"

Benicio nodded. "I know all the Hollywood ones now. The same guy is always outside my house *every* day so I just say hello and smile and make it as boring as possible so maybe one day he won't come. Then there are the ones at the nightclubs. They always try to make you react – saying something or getting close. They want you to be angry, you know? They can sell a shot of you looking mad for lots of money."

"Did you ever punch any of them?"

Benicio laughed at my question.

"Yeah, I did," he said. "One guy called Brian Pasadena. I was with a girl and he push her so I take his camera. He take hold of my hair like that," Benicio pulled a handful of his lush black hair and jerked his head backwards, "so I punch him in his face like that," he demonstrated an upper cut with this spare arm and laughed. "He deserve it. Then he swore he was going to get me back one day, but he never push any girl I am with again."

"Maybe it's him?" Ryan suggested with a smirk. "Maybe he's trying to get you back – sneak in and poison you or something."

Benicio laughed and shook his head. "I'm nothing special to him. That guy gets punched every week! All my friends have punched Brian Pasadena. No. Is more likely European paparazzi. Those guys are completely insane. They will risk their lives to get their photo."

It sounded so crazy. For a minute I felt sorry for celebrities who had these people camped outside their

110

houses or spying on their gardens with a long camera lens. Only for a minute, though. Benicio sounded like he had the right attitude for dealing with it.

Luce had finished his drink and was now bored with standing by the lake. He came over, stood directly in front of me and stared at me. His liquid eyes bore into mine and I stared back at him.

"Can I help you?"

Benicio laughed. "I think we'd better get going again," he said. "Your black beauty might do something to us if we don't."

Ryan tutted dismissively. "He's just being dramatic, Ben. Don't get taken in by him."

Luce snorted and shook his head toward Ryan. "He knows what you say," Benicio said. "In a minute he will turn you to stone."

I liked the idea Benicio seemed to have of Luce, like he was knowing and mystical. I stood up and put my arm under Luce's strong neck and leaned my head against him, taking a deep breath of his wonderful smell. Luce rested his head on my shoulder.

"Come on," Ryan said, stretching. "We've got a spooky clearing to find."

We reached the second clearing after another exhilarating gallop and stopped in the middle. As soon as the three of us were standing together, with the guys waiting for me to point them in the right direction, I felt a pang of anxiety. It was stupid and irrational and I pushed the feeling away. Had yesterday's eerie little journey really affected me that much? Something about the place had definitely left its mark. Ryan and Ben were waiting for me to speak and I felt another little quiver of anxiety in my chest. When I looked up at them they were both giving me a funny look.

"You okay?" Benicio asked.

I nodded, a lot, and smiled.

"Sure. The path is over there." I pointed over to where the narrow trail wound away from the large open space. From the center of the clearing, I couldn't even see a gap in the trees – and then suddenly I was struck with a new, stupid fear that we'd get there and the path just wouldn't be there at all and we'd search and search for it and then everyone would think I was crazy…

"We don't have to go back there if you don't want to."

It was Ryan who spoke, his dark eyes showing concern.

"Do I look scared or something?"

The boys spoke together. "Yes."

"You've gone pale," Ryan added.

"I just felt a bit funny at the thought of the place," I told them. "It's kind of scary on the way in… I can't describe it. You'll see… maybe. Or maybe you'll think I'm nuts."

Benicio reached out to me and placed his hand on my shoulder. "We are here this time," he said.

I nodded.

"Follow me."

As soon as I turned Luce and headed for the path my horse picked up the pace to a fast trot. He was urging to go to a higher gear but I wouldn't let him. Just like last time, he was the one who found the path. I was convinced we were heading for a wall of trees, but then I saw that one tree which looked like it was in the outer ring was actually set back from the others, and by slipping between it and the outer tree and turning to the right a bit, we got to the start of the path.

It was as narrow as I remembered and again, by the time we had walked ten yards along, the bright sunny clearing already seemed miles away. Luce walked forwards quietly and sensibly, showing no sign that he was thinking of acting up. The other two were close behind me.

"Cold," Benicio commented.

We walked on the gently curving path. The skeleton-like silver birches hung between the trunks of the larger trees and nothing broke the deathly silence except the methodical sound of hooves on grass, then a crack of snapping wood somewhere to the left. Red whinnied and must have reared up as I heard his front hooves pound down on the earth.

"All okay," Ryan called.

I turned to see Toby walking on regardless and had a moment where Luce tried to speed up on me. There was no one in the forest, I thought. It was just one of those unexplained woodland noises. The curving path continued, longer than I'd imagined it would feel the second time. Luce's dramatic behavior the day before had made it feel five miles long, and I was sure it was more like a hundred yards, but it wasn't. It was definitely a lot further. Then, finally, we were there and I led Benicio and Ryan to the center of the clearing.

"Hmm, that was fun," Ryan said, coming alongside. "I can see how you were a bit freaked, especially if he was acting up."

"It's good Toby's here," I replied. "The others stayed calm."

Benicio nodded and made a face. "I don't like those white trees," he said.

113

"Skeletons in the forest," I said.

"Exactly," Benicio replied.

We all looked around at the perimeter of the clearing, at the tall, ivy-choked poplars.

Ryan shrugged.

"There's nothing here, is there? Maybe this is just as far as they got before Luce shook them off and got away?"

He could have been right, but my instinct was that there was something to discover. Luce was snorting, and then he made an odd jump with his front hooves, stamping them down in close succession on the long, unkempt grass. Ryan gave me a funny look. Then Luce took a step forwards and did the same thing again. Of all the strange, silly and bizarre behavior I had ever witnessed from him, I'd never seen him do anything like this before.

I reached down and patted his neck reassuringly.

"You crazy fool," Ryan said, eyebrow raised. "He looks like he's trying to dance!"

"We could check out the perimeter," he suggested then. It seemed like a good idea. "Ben, why don't you see if there's anything over on that side," Ryan pointed vaguely to the edge of the clearing. "I'll go this way," he said to me, nodding in the opposite direction. "You stay here and see what he does."

"Yes sir," I joked. Ben and Ryan started to turn Red and Toby and make for the edges of the clearing, but as they did so, a strange sound reached our ears. It was the sound of hooves hitting something hollow. Benicio looked at both of us. Toby stopped. We watched as the huge gray lowered his head and stamped the ground with his right hoof, ever so gently. Whatever Toby and Benicio were standing on, it

114

wasn't solid ground. Toby wasn't happy and backed away slowly, as we shot each other open-mouthed glances.

"That sounds like wood," Ryan said, dismounting slowly and passing Red's reins to me.

As Benicio took Toby away to the side, Ryan stood where they had been and walked forwards, slowly, one step at a time, treading heavily. With his first two steps we heard nothing but the swishing sound of his feet in the grass. But then, the unmistakable thud of walking on wood.

Ryan stopped and stamped his foot again.

"Wood," he said. Ben and I nodded as I felt Luce tense his muscles and saw his ears go flat. Benicio dismounted, handed Toby's reins to Ryan and started tapping the ground to find the dimensions of whatever was beneath the grass.

"It's a door!" he said, his voice showing the exertion of hopping around on one leg. "A big door."

"Is there an edge?" Ryan sounded as excited as I felt. There *was* something here!

"Salma, take Toby and the others away a bit," He nodded to Luce. "He looks like he's about to freak out."

I suddenly felt like I was sitting on an unexploded bomb. Luce started shuffling sideways, and Red was getting the vibe from his friend.

I dismounted, reached out for Toby's reins, and retreated slowly with all three horses. Luce was grateful to be moving to the edge of the field and seemed to calm down a little. His eyes had started to go all over the place but now he looked straight at me, trusting.

I turned just in time to see Ryan and Benicio taking hold of something at ground level. They were bending down, about two yards apart. Then, with what looked like all

115

their strength, they hauled a square piece of the clearing upwards. I just had a chance to see the wooden underside of the trapdoor as it yawned open before I felt Luce's reins nearly jerk my arm out of its socket.

He recovered quickly once he realized I wasn't going to let go and the boys had let the trapdoor fall closed with another thud. I had to release the other two, but thankfully they remained close by. Ryan moved instantly toward Red and Toby and grasped their reins firmly. Benicio was there too.

"What's down there? Did you see?" My heart was pumping as I tried to take everything in.

"A shaft going down, with iron rungs in the wall," Ryan said breathlessly.

Benicio blew out a stream of air.

"We couldn't hold it," he said.

"Maybe our uninvited guests couldn't either." The thought came to me in a flash. "Maybe that's why they needed Luce, and the rope!"

"Maybe," Ryan replied. "I think we could have heaved it open, though. Did you see the way he was trying to tell us where it was with that jumping thing he did? Not such a fool after all, Luce. Sorry, dude!"

Luce snorted in response and we laughed.

"Now what?" Benicio asked.

"We come back," Ryan replied immediately.

I nodded. "Tomorrow. If we can get a break together."

"Definitely," Ryan again. He stole a glance at his watch and started. "Darn! Better get back. It's getting late."

Benicio looked at his watch and made a face too. "Wardrobe will kill me."

❉   ❉   ❉   ❉

117

Liv was waiting in the yard. Her face broke initially into a smile when she saw us coming around the corner from the paddock. But then she looked behind to where Benicio was bringing up the rear and her features turned to what I would describe as approaching panic.

"Don't tell me she's not with you!" Liv's eyes were wide and searching.

"Who?" We all asked together. But I knew who it would be.

"Rach didn't show up to meet Alex and she hasn't been seen since!"

Chapter Nine

Benicio raced off to grab a shower before reporting to wardrobe for the evening shoot.

"I won't say anything about the trapdoor!" he yelled over his shoulder before disappearing through the door in the castle wall. Liv told us her story first.

"She wasn't around the castle so I thought she must have gone off at the last minute with you three. We'd been in the spooky gallery and looked just in case Rach got in before us and got lost or something. Then we just stayed in there because I thought maybe Mr. V. had managed to drag her off to help or something like that. It's just like a maze and freaky with that bright blue carpet everywhere. There were dozens of doors we couldn't open. Alex was like a jailer jangling all these keys and trying them in every lock until we found the right one, if we were lucky. We only just came out of there. We saw the time and realized we'd been in there for two hours! I saw you hadn't come back so I came down here and assumed I'd see Rachel coming in with you."

"But she hasn't got a horse."

"I thought she might have taken Domino, because Hans took him for a ride this morning and I saw him heading back as I looked through one of the windows just before I went to meet Rachel and Alex. I thought she might have grabbed the chance to join you all on Domino. I wasn't too pleased that she'd gone off without telling me, though."

"She *would* have found you and told you," I said. Rachel wouldn't just go off and do something else if she'd already promised to meet someone.

Ryan nodded.

"There's no set supper time tonight because of the evening shooting schedule, so let's check our rooms again. You could have just missed her," he suggested. "She could even have gone for a spin with Steve in that sports car he rented."

"Yeah! Didn't think of that," Liv's features suddenly brightened. "Steve's crazy about Rach even though he knows she's got a boyfriend."

"Shouldn't he be here though, with the shoot starting soon?" I wondered.

"Yes," Ryan replied. "Let's check her room and then see if we can find Steve, or his car."

She wasn't in her room, and we couldn't spot Steve anywhere either. And when we saw the crew gathering for the evening shoot on the vast south terrace and saw no sign of him there we began to feel encouraged that Rachel might indeed have taken off with him for a drive in the car. She may have been going out with Tony, but that didn't mean Rachel didn't enjoy all the male attention. She got so much of it and she was just too nice to be rude.

"He should show up soon," Ryan said as we stood on the

120

corner of the patio, surreptitiously watching the growing activity as the crew set up the shots. Mr. Vazquez had gone off with Hans to a vineyard a few miles away, so we didn't have to worry about telling him anything. We agreed though, that if Steve appeared and hadn't seen Rachel we would have to raise the alarm.

I had the scary thought that Steve would tell us that he hadn't seen Rachel all day and I felt a rotten pang of fear in the pit of my stomach. I hoped I'd be wrong. I got a flash of Rachel's face as she looked up at the castle from the yard the day before and spotted the strange woman watching us. She had looked scared. I didn't want to say anything to the others. Not yet. But I had the feeling things were about to get complicated.

"Let's grab some supper while we can," Ryan suggested, nodding toward the open doors to the dining room.

We sat in a huddle at our usual table. I had my back to the door and watched as Ryan and Liv's eyes flicked up every time someone entered the room. I wondered if they were feeling as worried as I was about Rachel. My worry was growing with every minute that passed. If she was with Steve, what if they'd had an accident? I hoped Mr. Vazquez would be staying out all evening so we could find Rachel before he returned.

Then I remembered about the clearing and the trapdoor. Where did that all fit into everything? Did our uninvited paparazzi have anything to do with Rachel's absence? And who on earth was that strange woman who seemed to have gotten Alex all bothered?

"We need everyone together," Ryan said quietly as he finished his plate from the buffet. "When does Benicio finish?"

"Supposedly nine o'clock, but it could be ten or eleven. Who knows?"

"They shouldn't run long tonight." Ryan seemed certain. "They're just running dialogue. The start of Ella and David's great love affair," he laughed. Then I saw him look up and smile. It was Alex.

He sat down next to me. When he spoke, he looked only at Ryan and Liv.

"Have you found Rachel?"

Liv gave him an update and told him we were waiting for Steve.

"And we made an interesting discovery in the forest," Ryan announced.

Alex leaned in interestedly. "Really?"

"One of your secret tunnels." Ryan told him. "Or the end of one, anyway,"

Alex looked shocked.

"Wow! Can we go and take a look? Where?"

"The clearing Luce took me to yesterday." I replied. He almost turned to look at me properly. "There's an immense trapdoor just under the grass in the middle."

Alex looked back at Ryan and blew out some air. "Do you think someone was messing around there with Luce?"

We nodded. "He freaked when Benicio and I tried to open it," Ryan told him. "We saw rungs set into a wall though, going down."

Alex looked almost beside himself. "How would anyone know it was there, though?"

"Because they stole the plan of the castle," Liv replied shrugging.

"But if someone's attempting to get in, how would they be able to steal the plans in the first place?" I wondered aloud, "Unless there are two of them."

"Unless they have been coming in and out whenever they want," Ryan offered.

"But they needed your horse for something to do with the trapdoor," Alex almost looked at me.

"And they also needed a rope," I said.

"They must have needed the rope for something to do with the trapdoor," Ryan offered. "Maybe there are rungs missing... or the door is too heavy to stay open, like Benicio said, so they need to keep it pulled up."

"It's so nice that you have made some friends this week, Alex." The Count was standing at the end of our table. He looked exactly as he did the first night when he had made the speech. He smiled at us, strangely, but I think that was just his usual smile.

"Are you all enjoying your time here with us?" he asked. We all enthusiastically answered in the affirmative.

"It's wonderful, thanks," Liv told him. "It's so nice to meet Alex too," she went on.

Alex and the Count smiled as the father laid his hand on his son's shoulder.

"I have to take him away from you just now, I'm afraid." Alex was smiling politely but his face also told us it was the last thing he wanted.

"That's fine, father," he said. "I'll see you later," he told us, adding, "Text me or something."

When they had left the dining room we collectively heaved a sigh of relief.

"Do you think he heard what we were talking about?"

123

Liv asked. "He just appeared there like a ghost. He could have been there for ages, for all I knew."

I nodded. "He kind of freaks me out. We've hardly seen him. It's like he hides out somewhere most of the time."

"It's Alex's mom who frightens me," Ryan said. "She's like some dead 1950s movie star, and she looks like she needs a good meal." We all laughed quietly. "They're weird. And is it me, Salma, or is Alex being funny with you?"

I shrugged and made a face. So it *was* noticeable "Looks that way, but I haven't got a clue what I might have done."

"Hmm." Liv murmured and then her features twisted into anguish. "Oh, Rach! Where are you?!"

I went and took a shower. It was stomach-churning waiting for Steve to turn up and praying Mr. Vazquez wasn't about to pull up in Hans's car at any moment. I pulled on clean clothes and flung myself on the bed. The late evening summer sky was a fantastic blue.

The next thing I knew, I woke with a start. I looked at my watch. It was nine o'clock. I felt like I'd slept for years and scrambled off the bed to find the others. At the bottom of the narrow staircase up to our rooms I went crashing into Benicio and bounced off his shoulder.

"Sorry!"

"Salma! I'm sorry. We were just coming to look for you. Rachel's not back."

"Is Steve?"

"Yes. She wasn't with him at all."

Benicio took my arm and steered me down the corridor. "Ryan just got a text from her."

"What!?"

"They're waiting for us in the yard. Come on."

We raced down the staircase and across the landings as fast as we could, running into the yard where Ryan and Liv were tacking up Red, Toby, Luce and Velvet. Ryan stopped what he was doing and pulled his phone from his pocket.

"I was just coming to find you," he said, breathlessly. "Rach just sent this."

Ryan tapped on the buttons and presented the phone to me. It read *They have come back for them*.

"You sure it's her?"

"Has to be," Ryan replied. "Thank goodness for the phone tower the Count let the phone company put on the roof!"

I frowned and shook my head, really struggling to take everything in. It seemed a frantic plan had come together while I'd been asleep.

"It's strange that she didn't text 'help' or something more urgent," I mused.

"That's why we're going to try and find her before we have to tell anyone," Ryan said.

"We're going to the clearing," he nodded to Luce. "He's ready."

"What on earth does 'They have come back for them' mean!?" I asked as I took Luce's reins. "And where's Alex?"

"No idea…" Ryan started.

Just then we heard the sound of a heavy vehicle approaching on the gravel drive.

Ryan swore.

"That's Dad back with Hans!" We all looked at each other in a panic and I felt the adrenaline beginning to pump through me.

125

"Liv! Do anything to stall them until we come back. Say we've gone for a ride and you suddenly felt ill or something."

She was about to protest. "You *have* to! Please Liv," Ryan pleaded. "He'll believe you. Tell him we'll be back in an hour."

"Okay," Liv said as the noise of the engine and crunching gravel under the wheels grew louder. "I'll try and catch up. But you three just go! Now!"

I grabbed Luce's reins and drove him toward the corner of the yard as Ryan and Benicio did the same. I hoped Toby would be okay for him again, considering we were taking off at a much more frantic pace and the tension in the air was unmistakable. It would be dark soon. I didn't want to think about how soon.

A thought came to me as we turned to go along the back of the stable block.

I shouted to Ryan as quietly as possible and he turned and frowned as I drew alongside.

"Do you have the trailer keys on you?"

He nodded.

"Just give them to me for a second."

Without hesitation, Ryan took the keys from his pocket and passed them to me. I dismounted, gave him Luce's reins, then dashed back to the end of the wall and edged around enough to see if anyone was in the yard. It was empty. I sprinted across the gap at the corner to where the trailer was parked, next to the entrance to the paddock. I unlocked the door and I was in. The rope was exactly where it was supposed to be. I grabbed it, pulled the door closed with a click and relocked it, then raced back to Ryan and remounted.

He and Benicio looked at the rope and nodded.

We galloped to the edge of the second clearing and slowed to enter the narrow pathway that would take us to the small clearing. I decided Ryan should go first so Luce would see Red ahead of him if he freaked out. We started the walk along the cold, eerie path in silence.

I was still kicking myself for falling asleep and missing the whole discussion which had led to us visiting the clearing this late, as the light faded. It seemed to have been Benicio's idea but it had to have something to do with Rachel and her text. It had to. I had a thousand questions to ask the two boys, the first one being, "What on earth are we doing?"

My mind whirred and in no time we were on the final curve of the path. There wasn't time to be apprehensive about the denseness of the forest or the spookiness of the passage. Luce followed Red very steadily, probably because he didn't have me up there terrified out of my wits. I was calm and determined this third time and he clearly felt it, letting out a soft snort as we all drew level at the edge of the clearing.

We were confronted by total stillness. Ryan dismounted and Benicio and I followed suit. We stood in a huddle with our horses.

"Well done getting that rope," Ryan whispered.

"Thanks," I replied, whispering too. "I figured if *they* needed it then we might."

"What are we going to do?" Benicio shrugged.

We all looked at each other.

"Do you think we'll find Rach if we go down there? Is that why we're here?"

The boys nodded. Benicio spoke.

"Someone's been messing with the trapdoor. We think whoever it is has something to do with Rachel disappearing."

"That's kind of a leap in logic though, isn't it? To race out here?"

Then Ryan spoke. "She also wrote she's in the dark. It has to be the labyrinth or one of the secret passageways. We couldn't find Alex when we needed him, so we thought we'd just go for it and come out here – see what we could find." Then he added, "And Benicio has a hunch."

I looked at Benicio. His Hollywood eyes twinkled and he grinned.

I thought for a second.

"Her text was kind of weird, wasn't it? It was almost like she wanted us to try and find her."

Ryan continued where I left off. "Like she wanted us to solve this mystery," he said.

"Maybe no one has Rach at all. I mean, maybe she found the room where that woman was – the one off from the spiral staircase – and someone came in and she had to hide?"

"She'd only hide if she was scared though," Ryan said. "If we find her we'll find out what these people are up to. I'm sure of it."

"*They have come back for them.*"

The phrase kept running through my head. Rachel must have thought we would understand what she meant… we *should* understand what it meant…

"Do you still think it's paparazzi?" I asked Benicio. He shrugged his response. "I don't know," he replied.

I turned to look at the center of the clearing.

"Are you two going to open the door?"

They nodded. "Let's go," Ryan said.

I held three sets of reins and stroked three silky noses. Apart from a couple of tail swishes they all seemed okay. Benicio and Ryan found the trapdoor quickly and in no time they held a corner each and were heaving the door open. With a final push, it fell backwards past the vertical and thudded down against the grass. There was now a large square hole in the middle of the clearing. The boys had stood back but moved forward again to peer over the edge. Luce jerked his head up and flattened his ears. I stared into his beautiful eyes and then held him against me, talking into his ear.

Benicio squatted down and listened – Ryan too. Then Ryan started to disappear into the hole. My heart lurched with apprehension. He was the stuntman, after all! I suppose between the two of them, it had to be Ryan who went first. His head disappeared below the level of the grass, but only a few seconds later he reemerged and climbed fully out of the shaft.

The two of them came over to me.

"There are a lot of rungs missing," Ryan whispered. "And the ones that are there aren't much good. They wobble a lot. I had to be really careful."

"How far does it go down?" Benicio asked.

"Can't see."

"But now we know why they needed the rope," I said. "And why they needed him." I gestured to Luce.

The boys nodded slowly.

"You can't tie anything to those rungs," Ryan said.

"Why didn't they tie the rope to a tree? There are enough of them."

"Too far away?" Benicio offered.

He was right. You would have to have a very long rope to reach from the edge of the clearing. Obviously, our intruders, or whatever they were, didn't have one that long.

And neither did we.

"Toby will be alright," Ryan said. "He's done it before on a shoot a few years ago – bizarrely."

I untied the end of the rope from my belt.

Luce suddenly pushed forwards toward the center of the clearing. I stopped him after a few paces and turned back to the others.

"I think he has other ideas," I said. We all let out a quiet burst of laughter. Luce wanted to do it. He was a marvel. Suddenly I wanted him to do it.

"He's safe this time, and we won't do it the way they did. There's a better way." Ryan told us.

"Let's tie Toby and Red," he suggested and efficiently found a suitable side branch from a stray birch tree. "They'll be okay."

We walked to the center of the clearing with Luce and stopped. Ryan began to unravel the rope as Benicio and I listened at the mouth of the hole. Luce stood still next to the hole.

"He'll naturally want to pull with his shoulders so I'll tie it loosely around the base of his neck." Ryan started to place the rope over Luce. "Through the stirrups too, to keep it from slipping. We need to put it low over his shoulders so it doesn't interfere with his breathing."

Luce stamped the ground as the rope was set up, but he remained still. I watched him in awe. "He'll push his front feet forwards to take the strain of the weight." Ryan finished rigging up the rope. "This will be a lot better for him than what they tried when they brought him here. We will help take the strain. He's being really good, I can't believe it." Ryan gave Luce a friendly rub on his neck. Luce snorted a response.

"I'll do it," I said.

"What?" Benicio said.

"Sorry, darling," Ryan said, suddenly sounding masterful and very patronizing. "You're not going down there."

I returned his very definite glare. "It has to be me," he said firmly.

"I'm really light," I protested. "We have to do what's best for him. I'm less likely to pull the rungs out, too."

Ryan opened his mouth to speak and stopped. He let his shoulders drop and turned to Benicio.

"She's right," he conceded.

"I want to do it," I lied. "I'm not scared and it can't go on forever. My arms are strong too, so I could pull myself up on the rope if I have to. I won't do anything silly."

"We already are," Ryan countered. "What do you think, Ben?"

Benicio stared at me for a moment.

"You really want to do this?"

I nodded fiercely – realizing we were about to do another unplanned movie stunt.

"It's best for Luce."

"The minute you feel scared you shout up and we'll get you out," he said. "Promise?"

I nodded again and went over to Luce. He stood there in anticipation. Luce knew that we had to do this and I felt like crying as he remained calm and still – confronting a fresh trauma head on. He was a wonderful horse. I stepped away and he stared at me and I stared back.

"Okay," I said – and sat at the edge of the hole. If I hadn't moved then I wouldn't have been able to tear myself away from my horse's solemn liquid gaze. I wanted to stay with him and at the same time I wanted to run a million miles from where I was – but I pushed the fear aside. Taking hold of the first rung, I turned myself around and placed my foot on one further down, testing its strength. There was one past that which took my head down into the shaft. I looked down and saw only one more rung. Ryan lowered the rope in. I took it surely with one hand and gently increased my weight on it.

"Go on," Ryan called. "We're okay here."

I took hold of the rope with my other hand. The rungs above me kept it away from the side so I could grip it without scraping my hands against the wall of the shaft. I pushed one foot against the wall and then the other, taking all my weight on my arms. I wanted to kiss Tony for forcing me to do chin-ups on the doorway to my little balcony at home. He had teased me for being weak and counted repetitions until I could easily hang there and do as many chin-ups as I liked.

I half expected the rope to suddenly give way. It didn't. Luce had clearly not moved an inch since taking my weight. I lowered myself as nimbly as I could into the darkness. No rungs appeared on the wall in front of me so I just kept going. A damp, peaty smell engulfed me and I heard a trickle of water from somewhere. The light from above was enough to show me the detail of the wall and the bricks. This was a properly built shaft, more than two yards wide. It was no ordinary hole in the floor. It had to lead somewhere important. I looked up and saw Benicio peering down at me.

It must have been four or five yards since the last rung when my foot found solid ground. I had reached the bottom of the shaft. I turned in the blackness and gave a little start as behind me I found a doorway. There was no door. It was the beginning of a long, dark tunnel and my sense of direction told me that it led off in the direction of the castle.

I called up to the boys, "I'm at the bottom. There's a passage!"

I took a deep breath. "I'm going to go down it."

I could just make out the brick paved floor as it started off, but for all I knew it could have disappeared into an endless chasm. After a few steps into the passage it was impossible to see anything ahead of me. I felt ahead with my foot, my hands flat against the sides, and took two further steps in. Then I heard a noise, not from behind me, but from the tunnel. It was footsteps. Someone running – straight toward me!

Chapter Ten

I backed out of the passageway and flattened myself against the side of the shaft wall, frozen by fear.

Benicio and Ryan were staring down at me, looking concerned. I called up to them in an urgent whisper.

"Someone's coming!"

Ryan's head disappeared for a moment.

"Wait five seconds and then take the rope and get out!" he called.

I waited. I could feel my heart pounding and the footsteps were drawing closer. I needed to get up that rope fast and hoped I wouldn't put too much stress on Luce in my urgency. I finished counting to five and stepped forward to grasp the rope. But something made me turn and look down the tunnel.

I knew those footsteps. It was the click-clack of beach shoes – Rachel's beach shoes – the ones she lived in all summer!

She burst through from the darkness of the tunnel and her mouth dropped open at the sight of me standing in the shaft. Three seconds later she was next to me.

"They're behind me. We've got to get out of here!" she said.

"You go first," I urged.

"No, you!" she insisted. "I'll be quick!"

Ben and Ryan were peering down at us – a mixture of elation and confusion etched on their faces.

"We're coming!" I shouted. I waited for a few more seconds until I thought Ryan would be with Luce and began to climb the rope, hand over hand as fast as I could. Luce was doing a fantastic job of keeping the rope still. I reached the last rung in a few seconds and took hold of one as high above me as I could reach, scrambling onto the next, and then my feet searched and found the last one to stand on. Benicio helped me out of the shaft. Luce whinnied a greeting as if he was just minding his own business in the paddock. I'd just caught sight of his front legs splayed forwards as he leaned back, his hooves digging in and his neck taking the strain on the rope. Now he stood up again, calm and still and shook his head dramatically. I wanted to hug him forever.

"Okay!" I shouted down to Rach.

"Three seconds!" Benicio called. "Then come."

Luce felt the weight once again on the rope and dug his front hooves in. Benicio grabbed hold of the rope in order to take some slack away from Luce. I did the same as we felt Rachel's weight pull on the other end.

In a few seconds she called, "I'm on the rungs," and we felt the rope go slack.

Benicio and I scrambled forwards to help her out of the shaft. Rachel stood and hugged her brother as I took hold of Luce and gave him a kiss. He nickered at me.

"Wow! Have you been doing weights or something?!" Ryan exclaimed. Rachel laughed exhaustedly.

"Tony makes me do chin-ups," she said. I wanted to laugh my head off but there wasn't time.

"They're after me," Rachel gasped. "They'll be right down there any second."

We all looked down into the hole. As Ryan yanked the rope upwards two people came crashing out of the darkness against the wall. One, a man, made a vain attempt to jump and grab the end of the rope as it whipped upwards. I knew his face, I was certain I did. He was middle-aged – tired looking – and I thought I recognized the face of the lady standing beside him. I guessed it was Rachel's scary woman. She was thin and her face was gaunt. Her hair was blonde and pulled off her face. The pair of them didn't look to me much like photographers, even photographers in disguise – and they certainly weren't ghosts.

They then realized that there were three of us peering in at them and that they had no way of escape. Then they turned and rushed back down the tunnel.

Ryan was pushing buttons on his cell phone and undoing the knot on the rope around Luce.

"Alex? We've got Rachel – at the trapdoor! She was being chased and now they've gone back down the tunnel. We need to figure out where it comes out. Call security and tell them to meet us at the second clearing in a few minutes and we'll show them the shaft."

"I'll go," I told him. Luce was free from the rope and I took his reins. "You guys stay here."

I mounted up and we were off. Luce took the passage

out of the clearing much faster than I would have liked, but I let him go and enjoyed the crazy ride.

If you've ever waited for help you'll know that those few minutes feel like a lifetime. Luce and I stood twenty or so yards away from the passage to the clearing. I spent the time talking to him and patting his neck affectionately. He was a total star. The calm quiet of the surrounding trees betrayed nothing of the drama unfolding and the adrenaline pumping through my veins. I felt the darkness creeping over us.

After what seemed like forever, I heard the four-wheel drive vehicle, and then it emerged from the main trail. They spotted me and drove across the space, coming to a sudden halt. Luce didn't move a whisker as four huge security guards in black bomber jackets jumped out. Each carried a flashlight, which in a short while would be badly needed.

I pointed to the start of the passage.

"Through there. Just follow the path."

Luce and I turned and headed across the clearing. I was heading for the trail as usual, but my horse definitely had other ideas. Seeming to sense the urgency, Luce was making straight for the trees. I felt a kind of apprehensive gulp in my chest and urged him on, my trust in what he was about to do unquestionable. Luce liked riding through trees. He liked to pick his way – fast. I shouldn't really have let him go for it – there were dangers, but it would save time. I knew he was sure where he was going, and before I could wonder if it really was a good idea we were already in the woods. The tall trees were dotted like an obstacle course with hardly any smaller birches or bushes in between.

Luce pressed on with relish and I hung close over his neck, weaving with him, gripping his sides with my ankles, moving as one and letting him take me through. We were surrounded on all sides but we were headed in the right direction. Just when I thought we would collide with a trunk in the fading light, Luce picked his way beautifully around it. It was a skillful maneuver and he undertook it with his usual brashness. He was truly a stunt horse in the making. The wide trunks flew past on either side, and suddenly we burst out onto the trail. We'd shaved off a good part of the way back and saved precious time.

Then, flying out of the twilight came Domino, with Hans on board. Now I was even more confused. What was he doing coming back in on Domino when about half an hour ago he'd returned with Mr. Vazquez from their trip to the vineyard? Hans slowed and reined in as he saw me, his eyes wide with surprise.

"What's going on?"

I told him as fast as possible, about Rachel disappearing, the whole story. It was when I mentioned the text that Hans's expression began to change to one of enlightenment.

"I went out to try and find you all," he told me. "There was something in the way little Liv looked… come with me," he said, "I think I know how we can catch them. I've already disabled their getaway car."

"What car?"

"The one I just found in the forest," he replied, "in exactly the same place they parked it thirty years ago."

He turned to Domino as the light switch flicked on in my head.

I *did* know the faces peering up at me out of the shaft. I'd seen them staring out of the newspaper clippings.

They have come back for them. The jewels!

Alex's wonderful story flooded back. His Uncle Philip, and Sofia the servant girl. They had stolen the jewels and been discovered as they tried to make their escape. The jewels were never found – hidden for decades somewhere in the castle. Now Uncle Philip was back to retrieve them. The face staring up at me from the shaft was Alex's Uncle, unmistakable from the photo the newspaper had used. Much older, but unmistakable.

Luce and I flew down the trail after Domino and Hans as the dusk finally closed in. As we reached the yard Liv was there with Chokky and Velvet – and Alex. Hans and I dismounted and tied the horses.

"Come with me," he ordered Alex. "Liv, please look after the horses. Salma, you must come too as you have seen them and can identify them." I nodded.

I was beginning to feel sorry for Liv being bossed around and missing all the fun.

She nodded.

"Okay!"

Alex and I raced after Hans to the door in the castle wall.

As we pelted up the stairs to the first landing, I listened to Hans filling Alex in. But it was my guess that Alex had almost worked it out for himself. He knew the woman's face didn't fit. He'd been so intrigued by Rachel's story and he had been on to something.

We tore up the staircases and along corridors until we reached the fourth floor. Suddenly I knew where we were heading. I followed Hans and Alex into the south wing.

139

"I knew I'd seen her face," Alex said, as we reached the door through to the private drawing room. "I checked the newspaper cuttings from thirty years ago and I was almost certain when I saw the pictures. But my father came into the library as I was looking, so I had to shove them back onto the shelves. He wouldn't want me searching for anything to do with what happened. I had to be sure it was them before I said anything."

So now I knew why the file of clippings we'd found was all jumbled up.

We followed Hans through and diagonally across to the paneled corridor which doubled back toward the courtyard windows and the music room, then the door to the library.

Hans retrieved the key from the window ledge, just as Ryan had done, and unlocked the door. We entered the wonderful room.

"What are we doing here?" Alex asked. "Do you know something I don't?"

Hans nodded. His eyes crinkled up in that lovely way as he smiled.

"I know that tunnel," he said. "I turned the place upside down looking for the jewels for your father after they escaped all those years ago. I wanted to be the one who returned them to him."

He headed over to the huge sofas and the fireplace surrounded by the bookcases on either side. Alex and I followed.

"I know the twists and turns in there like the back of my hand," Hans continued.

"The passage takes them into the castle through the spiral stairs."

"What spiral stairs?" Alex frowned.

"They are connected to the labyrinth," Hans went on. "From there, you can get anywhere."

"Rachel found them," I told Hans. "She got lost in there and was trying all the doors. She ended up on a spiral staircase and was totally lost when some woman –"

"Sofia."

"Yes. It must have been her. She opened a door to the spiral staircase and pulled Rachel through into a room, with just a mattress in it and no windows."

"I know that room," Hans nodded. "They must have the main bunch of keys to all the doors in there. They could have been back at the castle for weeks waiting for their chance to get the jewels and escape, probably while we were all distracted with the movie shoot!"

"And Rachel got in the way – twice!" Alex interjected. "I bet she got into the labyrinth when we were supposed to meet her and bumped into them again."

"I think she did," I told him. "Unlucky her."

Alex looked straight at me and smiled. He turned to Hans.

"So why are we here in the library?"

Hans lifted his index finger to us. "Watch," he said and stepped forward to the bookcase directly to the left of the huge sandstone fireplace. He reached his hand out and carefully took hold of the red leather spine of a book on the shelf at about shoulder height. He paused for a moment. I held my breath as he pushed the book inwards. As he did so, there was a clicking sound and the shelf pivoted at the center. Alex and I followed Hans as he stepped forwards. Through the gap that had appeared were a small, wooden landing and the top of a winding staircase.

Alex clapped his hand to his forehead.

"I can't believe it," he said and blew out a long stream of air. "I never knew!"

"Your father didn't want you to – or anyone else," Hans told him. "This is for emergencies."

"I've lived here my whole life. I played in here when I was a kid. I can't believe I didn't know the biggest secret the castle ever had." Alex was breathless with surprise.

"I'll be back in one moment," Hans told us. "If you hear anyone coming up, close the bookcase."

He dashed across the library and back to the door. Alex turned to me. "I knew there were passages I didn't know about, but this is amazing," he said in a whisper. I smiled back at him.

Alex looked me in the eye and sighed.

"I'm sorry, Salma," he said. "I've been awful to you the last day or two."

My smile turned to a frown.

"We were getting along so well," I told him. "Did I say something wrong?"

He shook his head.

"I saw you and Ryan."

"What do you mean?"

"On the landing in the dark… I saw you together."

My face flushed hot at the memory. The person who had walked past as Ryan kissed me – was Alex. It hadn't even been a real kiss… Was it worth explaining it to Alex? I looked at his gorgeous face. He was staring back at me. I could see he was hurt and it was my fault. He really liked me and he had stumbled on me kissing someone else. I could see it all in his beautiful green eyes.

143

"It's not what you think… No, really," I finished firmly, as Alex's shoulders dropped. "We were sneaking around and we suddenly heard you coming so we panicked and that was Ryan's idea of how to not look suspicious. I hope you believe me."

Why was I trying so hard to convince him?

"He's crazy about you. Any idiot can see that. No wonder he took his chance." Alex laughed to himself.

I felt my heart leap at his words. "But we're not together," I told him. "We never have been."

I was getting muddled again. The choice was suddenly right before me. There was lovely, kind, genuine Alex. And there was Ryan, moody and a bit mysterious.

I jumped out of my skin as we heard the sound of hurried footsteps racing up the spiral staircase from far below. Alex and I looked at each other in terror. It was them! What on earth were we supposed to do? Let them get out through the mysterious room with no window – or make it into the library? Where was Hans?!

He came rushing back into the room. My eyes nearly popped out of my head as I saw that in his right hand he brandished a beautiful, long, steel sword. He must have grabbed it from a coat of armor on one of the landings. Alex was gaping too.

"I'm not losing my other eye to these too," he said solemnly to Alex.

Alex nodded hurriedly. "They're coming up the stairs."

"Stay here," he ordered us. Hans slipped through the bookcase and down the stairs.

I closed my eyes. Any minute, I was sure we would hear a bloodcurdling scream or a gunshot. It felt like I was in the middle of a movie climax. Hans was like a man possessed. It was as if he had been waiting for this moment all of his life. There was enjoyment in his eyes as he disappeared down the stairs. I just wanted to see him again in one piece.

"What should we do?" I asked Alex, as the panic threatened to take over.

"Hide behind the sofa," he suggested. "If they make it through it'll be up to us. We'll have to surprise them."

That was what I had been afraid of. The sounds of a scuffle echoed through the open bookcase. A scream and then…

"Aaaarghh!"

Was it Hans? I thought my heart would pop out of my chest as I crouched down behind the massive sofa. Alex was behind the one facing it. Then there was the sound of footsteps rushing up the stairs to the top, the scraping of soles on wood. Louder and louder. One set of footsteps. And now they were through the gap and into the library. Alex broke his cover.

"You're not going anywhere!"

"That's what you think."

I peered up above the back of the sofa and saw Sofia standing there. She was dressed in a maid's uniform and facing Alex. She was short and very thin. Her blonde hair was piled above her head in an old-fashioned style.

"*You* have no right to be the heir of Lindenberg Castle anyway," she said breathlessly. Her voice was rasping – mean.

"And you do?" Alex challenged her. He stared, wide-eyed and determined. "You're nothing but a thief. You and stupid Uncle Phillip. I knew it was you two. You'll get what you deserve this time."

145

The book on the bottom shelf, right next to where I was crouching, was huge, like a big black slab.

"I can see you've got what you came for," Alex nodded at her waist and then I saw it too. A small, red velvet gem bag.

It had to be the lost jewels. There was silence from the staircase. I reached for the big black book and took hold of the spine with one hand. The books on either side of it were smaller, so it was easy to slide out – and more importantly, completely silent. I took the weight of the book without looking at what I was doing. My eyes were fixed on Sofia. She had no idea I was there.

Then, just to add to the tension, slow, heavy footsteps began to ascend the staircase. Whose, I obviously had no idea. My heard pounded like never before.

I seized my moment as Alex and Sofia peered through the bookcase. I sprung up from behind the sofa. The weight of the book nearly snapped my arm as I tried to bring it up with me. I flung it, with the strength of my bicep, like a short putter, just as Sofia spun around to me, sensing my sudden movement. I got a flash of her mean face and its look of surprise before the flying book blocked my vision and hit her temple. She fell back on the sofa in front of Alex. Out cold.

One down, maybe one to go.

The footsteps labored upwards. All Alex and I could do was wait. He was in a better position to see through the bookcase than I was. *Please let it be Hans*, I screamed silently in my head.

One more step. Then another. Alex bent down over the unconscious Sofia and nimbly untied the jewel bag from her belt.

Another step.

Alex's shoulders relaxed and he closed his eyes with relief. Hans walked into the library. I saw an angry purple bruise on his cheekbone. He still carried the sword. There was blood on it so I didn't look again.

Alex rushed forward and hugged the older man.

"Thank goodness!" he cried.

I watched the tender embrace and it struck me – Hans was probably more of a father to Alex than the Count had ever been. Alex's eyes were closed as he hugged Hans tightly.

"I'm okay," Hans assured him. They both turned to me.

"Thanks for that," Alex said.

"No problem," I told him.

"What about Uncle Phillip?"

Hans sighed. "Just a flesh wound. He was reaching for his knife. I've tied him up, but we need security."

Alex reached for his phone as Hans collapsed onto the sofa in front of me.

I think I almost began to breathe normally again. Sofia wasn't about to come around any time soon.

When Alex finished summoning help he sat down next to Hans.

"These are for you," he said, producing the red velvet bag. "You can finally give them to my father."

Hans nodded slowly and took them. "I suppose they will never tell us where they hid them," he said and smiled.

Chapter Eleven

The security guards were fast, and ready when Sofia woke. The police had been called – and an ambulance. I'll remember the sound of her screaming and shouting as she was led out of the library and away through the castle for a long time.

Alex and I followed the guards down the spiral staircase with Hans leading the way. Uncle Phillip was in the room with no window. It was through the third door we reached. He was slumped against the wall. His hands and feet were tied with a torn sheet and his shoulder wound had been bound too. Hans had been busy in the moments after his strike with the sword.

The Count's brother looked old and finished. He put up no resistance when he was lifted to his feet and led slowly back up to the library. I took a good look at his face, so old and sad compared to the proud photo in all the newspaper articles. Somehow, I felt sorry for him.

Hans stood in the doorway with us as Philip was taken back up the stairs. He moved to follow.

"We're just going to take a look," Alex said, nodding down the winding staircase and brandishing a flashlight.

Hans smiled.

"See you later."

We descended the staircase. It took forever, passing door after door, down further and further, winding around and around until we reached a brick lined area. It was like an underground foyer and smelled just a little dank, like a cellar. Leading away from it were five passageways. Alex and I searched all around for a few moments with the aid of the flashlight beam.

"I think most of them just go under the castle to different points, like the kitchen. There's a big trapdoor under the dining room too," Alex said. "But one must lead to the clearing."

I nodded. "We could get lost. And we have no idea which direction we're facing. Let's just pick one and see where it goes."

"We could ask Uncle Phil which one it is," Alex laughed. "Okay. You pick one, and if it doesn't lead straight out we'll just turn back. I don't want to get lost either."

We stood in silence for a moment, the choices all around us. Then something happened before our eyes. A figure – a man, took shape before us – quickly. Suddenly he was there. He was quite old – with a long face and a big moustache and wearing clothes from about a century ago. It sounds corny, but he was a bit blurry around the edges. I felt Alex take my hand and neither of us moved. We both knew what we were seeing.

"Charles." I heard Alex whisper.

His great, great grandfather. The castle's more illusive ghost. I couldn't take my eyes off him, the silk waistcoat…

neat hair and calm features. Charles raised his arm and pointed down the passage directly in front of us. As it was clear where we should go, his image faded and was gone.

Alex and I let out a long breath. "That was unbelievable…" he trailed off.

I blinked and gave my head a little shake. There was no question that we'd just seen a one hundred percent real ghost.

"I think that's the one," I said, nodding directly ahead. We moved forwards.

"Wait! Salma…" Alex said. He was still holding my hand. "Maybe in another place at another time … maybe things could have been nice for us. I messed things up and I'm sorry."

He was wrong. It was me who had messed things up. I opened my mouth to speak. Alex shook his head.

"No. Don't worry. It's not often that people come here. And it's practically never that anyone as nice as you and your friends come to visit."

"It'll be different when the guests start to come," I told him. I just wanted to cry. The rest of us would all be leaving, but we'd have each other. Alex would be left on his own again, with only Hans for a companion.

"I should have just told you I liked you," Alex said, staring down at the brick floor.

I held his hand. It was all so, well… nice! I just turned to him and smiled.

We headed into the passageway and the darkness swallowed us up for a moment before Alex shone the flashlight forwards. We walked side by side. I let my free hand brush against the dry brick wall. The passage yawned out ahead of us.

"I think this is the one," Alex said after a while. "Good old Grandpa Charles! Did that really happen? Phew! We must be well outside the castle walls by now."

We stared ahead and eventually the flashlight beam picked out the end of the tunnel – and the shaft down from the clearing.

With a few yards to go, Alex squeezed my hand and then let it go. I turned and smiled at him and then stepped out into the moonlit shaft and looked up. Ryan's face stared down at us.

Relief swept his features. Then Liv, Benicio and Rachel were looking down at us too and the shouting started – exclamations and questions.

"Any chance of the rope being tossed down to us so we can get out?" I asked, when there was finally a brief period of silence. "Then we'll tell you everything,"

"Coming down in a second," Ryan shouted. "It's Toby's turn this time!"

Alex proved to be an agile rope climber as well. I hugged Toby when I got myself up, and then everyone else, and we all walked home in the bright, pale moonlight.

Rachel told us how, before she was due to meet Alex, she had decided to have a look for the windowless room. After some searching over on the far side of the south wing, she had found it – and the door had been open. She walked through the room to the spiral staircase upon seeing that door open too. She went down the stairs and then, to her horror, heard voices above in the room. Then the door to the stairs was shut and locked. Rachel listened as Uncle Philip and Sofia helpfully discussed everything to do with making their escape with the jewels – through the tunnel and to the car they had managed somehow to hide in the forest. After a while, Rachel tried to get out through the labyrinth, but found she was locked in. She frantically sent the text message and waited. But then she was discovered. She raced down the spiral staircase to the bottom and it was by pure chance that she chose the passage that led to the clearing and her eventual escape, using the light from her cell phone to just make out her way.

It had been an amazing evening. Benicio jogged off ahead of us as we reached the last stretch of the trail.

"I'll make some cell phone calls," he said, turning back, "then I'll get a table on the patio and we can all hang out."

That sounded like a good idea to us so we promised we'd see him there as soon as we finished up. I badly needed to sit down.

In the yard, Luce whinnied a greeting to us. Hans had untacked him and his coat looked like pure black gloss under the yard lights. We arrived just as the ambulance and the armored black police van pulled away slowly under the archway.

"I don't think they'll be coming back this time," Alex sighed.

Mr. Vazquez and Hans were watching the vehicles leave, and then they walked over to us. Rachel hugged her dad and he nodded at us all proudly. Hans's crinkly smile was back, lessening the effect of the purple bruise. He stood before us and took a deep breath.

"How can I thank you all?" he said. "Without you we'd never have found them, and I've been wanting to close this chapter of the castle's history for thirty years. I knew they would come back one day."

Hans touched his bruised cheek and sighed. I didn't want him to cry, but he looked like he might be about to. He reached into his pocket and his hand emerged clasping the little velvet bag. He looked at Alex.

"I'll tell the police about this little piece of evidence tomorrow. Now, I'm going to see your father."

I think we all wanted to hug him.

Alex nodded. He hugged Hans again before the older man walked away toward the main entrance.

We set about looking after the horses. Mr. Vazquez hung around for a few minutes, checking tack for the following day. Then he told us he was going to have a drink with Hans. We weren't the only ones who had made new friends at the castle.

Ryan settled Red down and then helped me with Luce.

"What a day!" he sighed.

"I knew something was going to happen here," I told him and smiled. "Alex was so close to cracking the mystery."

I didn't want to tell Ryan that Alex had seen us together.

"You know who the real hero is?" Ryan asked. My head spun. Did he mean himself? Was he jealous of what I'd just said about Alex?

"Our boy here," he patted Luce's neck. I sighed with relief as Luce snorted and stared down to the side.

I placed my arms over his back, rested my cheek against his side and breathed in the smell of him.

"I know," I said and I stayed like that for a while with my fantastic horse.

We waited for Alex to finish with Domino and waved goodbye to our beauties. As our footsteps crunched down the driveway a chorus of whinnies reached our ears, making us all laugh.

Rachel put her arm around my shoulder.

"The police will talk to us tomorrow," she told me, "after our shoot."

"Are you all ready for it?" Alex asked.

"Can't wait," I replied.

Alex smiled at me with a little twinkle in his eye.

We rounded the corner onto the now lively patio and saw Benicio waiting for us, dressed in a crisp black t-shirt that hugged his muscled arms. I grinned to myself and decided not to spend any more time worrying about boys.

Benicio waved and smiled. As we strolled over to join him I once again felt like I was walking into a scene from a movie.

One adventure was finished and tomorrow, another one would begin.